High School Sex Club

LAWRENCE BLOCK
writing as Andrew Shaw

A LAWRENCE BLOCK PRODUCTION

CLASSIC EROTICA

21 Gay Street
Candy
Gigolo Johnny Wells
April North
Carla
A Strange Kind of Love
Campus Tramp
Community of Women
Born to be Bad
College for Sinners
Of Shame and Joy
A Woman Must Love
The Adulterers
Kept
The Twisted Ones
High School Sex Club
I Sell Love
69 Barrow Street
Four Lives at the Crossroads
Circle of Sinners
A Girl Called Honey
Sin Hellcat
So Willing

Classic Erotica #16

High School Sex Club

Lawrence Block

CHAPTER 1

There is not a hell of a lot happening in Palmer, Massachusetts. There is the plant where the bulk of the residents of Palmer work diligently at the task of turning leather into shoes. There were other plants as well, but after the war the textile mills moved south to hunt up cheap labor, disdaining the strong unions and proud workingmen of New England. There is the plant, and there are the houses that contain the 7500 inhabitants of the town of Palmer. There are the public buildings around the square in the heart of town and there are two schools, the grade school and Nathan Palmer High School.

Nathan Palmer High School is the last contact the bulk of Palmer's youth has with the town. After graduation the ones with brains and/or money move on to college out of town. The ones who lack either brains or money or both get work, but they rarely get it in Palmer. Unless a boy has a business of his father's to step into, his economic opportunities are severely limited. After he graduates from high school he leaves the town, as often as not, and looks around for a larger city where he can get a better job and earn a better salary.

Nathan Palmer High School is a red-brick edifice large by Palmer standards. The cornerstone was laid in 1879 and the building was completed shortly thereafter. The high school fronts on Marshall Drive and rises an overpowering three stories into the rarefied air. The grounds are well kept, the grass green, the brick walls in a good state of repair. Periodically a window or two is broken but otherwise the building, from the outside, presents the appearance of a quiet and stately citadel of learning.

The students look like the stereotype of the adolescent in a television situation comedy. Freshly scrubbed, neatly dressed, smiling and a little awkward in an adult world. The urban brand of juvenile delinquency typified by ducktail haircuts and black leather jackets has not yet penetrated to Palmer from Boston or New York, and the clean and innocent appearance of the student body in general blends well with the quiet and stately appearance of Nathan Palmer High School.

In his office on the first floor of the school Samuel Pierce is busy going over seating plans and registration figures. He is the principal of Nathan Palmer High School, a soft little man whose family has lived in Palmer for eight generations. He wears wire-rimmed eye glasses and, when he is reading something very carefully, or pretending to himself that what he is reading demands careful attention, he has a marked tendency to squint.

What he is reading now is purely routine but he is squinting nevertheless, endowing the annual red tape with some sort of mystical importance. Another year has begun, another summer vacation has come to a regrettable finish, and Samuel Pierce once again must make some show of earning the $7200 he is paid annually for serving the school as its principal.

In her classroom on the third floor Miss Muriel Lynch rings an imitation Senegalese dinner-bell to summon her homeroom to order. The dinner-bell, which she believes to be genuine, is a souvenir of a trip to Paris which she took fourteen summers ago. This summer she has gone not to Paris but to a refined resort in Northern New Hampshire where she spent a very pleasant four weeks. She is thinking, as she rings the bell mechanically, that it is a great shame the summer turned out as it did. She had hoped secretly, to be sure, but just as fiercely as if she had shouted it from the rafters that that nice history teacher from Pawtucket had wanted her as more than a dinner companion and conversational partner. She had wished, as she wished each and every summer, for a romantic courtship leading to marriage. On occasion she had been known to settle for a brief summer affair, but this summer she was not even permitted that much. No, John Harper had wanted only her conversation, and she wondered sickly if anyone anywhere would ever want more than that from her for the rest of her life.

We could go on like this. Each room has a teacher, and at this time of the year each teacher is more in tune with her own private thoughts of the summer and of the coming year than with the class of neatly dressed and well-scrubbed pupils sitting before her. But let's forget the teachers for the time being. They are old, most of them, and not even their pasts are particularly interesting. The students, on the other hand, are young and far more alive. Obviously they are all ready to plunge back into the excitement of academic pursuit after three months from their books. Obviously they are all clean-minded young men and women with high ideals and a good measure of deserved self-respect.

Obviously.

•   •   •

Mary Hobson was not a beautiful girl.

In the black-and-white value pattern of Hollywood films and slick magazine articles, one might assume that Mary Hobson was therefore unattractive. Nothing could be further from the truth. She was an extremely attractive girl, with soft lustrous brown hair held by a rubber band in a long pony tail. Her eyes were large and brown, her features even and her skin the color and texture of rich whipping cream.

She was not beautiful for the simple reason that she was only seventeen years old. When she grew up she would possess the beauty that only a mature woman can have; at seventeen she was young and lovely and eminently desirable, but only a schoolboy as young as she was could have called her beautiful.

Her body had already matured. Her full breasts filled the pale yellow blouse she wore and her hips and buttocks were a bit too big for last year's red plaid skirt that she was wearing. She was a popular girl—a pretty girl whose prettiness was not at all flashy, a bright girl who was not "brainy," a good student without being a grind. At seventeen she was a senior; in June she would graduate, whereupon she would either go off to Boston College or marry Ed Bainbridge.

When the bell rang at the end of first hour history class her thoughts were not on college or marriage. She thought instead of Bonnie Leigh. Bonnie was her best girlfriend and the two of them hadn't been together since school got out in June. She and Ed had had a chance to get jobs together as junior counselors at Camp Picochee in Maine and Bonnie had remained in town, and Mary was anxious to get together with the other girl and compare notes. They had grown apart in the last year, probably because

Bonnie was going steady with Chuck Folsom and Ed and Chuck weren't friendly.

She caught Bonnie by the second-floor water fountain. Bonnie was cute rather than pretty, a girl whose popularity had been built more upon her vivacity and friendliness than her features. She was short and slender, with her black hair arranged in a Dutch cut.

And she was glad to see Mary.

"Welcome home, stranger," she said. "How does it feel to get back to civilization?"

"I guess it's good to be back. But it was good to get away. This is the best summer I ever spent, Bonnie."

"Up at Camp Whatchamacallit?"

"Camp Picochee. It was wonderful, Bonnie. I helped one of the senior counselors with a cabin of girls and I took charge of the nature group during activity periods. It was just great."

"Ed was there too, wasn't he?"

Mary nodded. "That's what made it so great. Oh, it would have been fun anyway, but being there with him—well, you know what I mean."

"Sure."

"It's such a great camp. It costs an absolute fortune for the kids to go there, you know. They have boating and hikes and canoe trips into the wilderness for the kids who are old enough and everything."

"You and Ed get to go on any of those trips?"

"Once. We assisted on a trip down Mannequois Creek toward Letchworth. It was . . . well, pretty romantic. We had a lot of time to ourselves."

Bonnie smiled. She didn't say anything, but Mary got the feeling there was something behind the smile that she couldn't pin down.

"I felt sorry for you," she said. "Just staying in the city. You must have been bored stiff."

"Not really."

"But what was there to do? Did you get a job?"

"Are you kidding? With all the kids out of school there weren't any jobs open."

"You must have gone out of your mind."

"Not me. I had plenty of fun, Mary. More fun than I ever had before."

"What did you do?"

Bonnie hesitated. Finally she said: "I don't know whether or not I should tell you."

"What—"

"Look," she said, "I'll tell you, but you've got to promise not to tell anybody. Is it a promise?"

"Sure."

"Not even Ed?"

"Okay."

Bonnie hesitated again. A bell rang and Mary shifted impatiently—they only had another minute or two to get to their next class. Mary's second-hour class was intermediate algebra and Mr. Chalmers was an absolute bear on the subject of getting to class on time.

"Hurry up," she urged.

"I'll tell you the rest of it later," Bonnie said. "First just answer me one thing. Did you and Ed ever go the limit? I mean all the way?"

"Of course not!"

"Well," said Bonnie, "I did."

Mary opened her mouth. She didn't know whether or not to believe it.

"I'm not kidding, Mary."

"With—with Chuck?"

Bonnie nodded.

"But—"

"I'll tell you one thing more," Bonnie said, turning to go. "It wasn't just with Chuck. It was with a lot of boys and it was wonderful."

Mary's mouth dropped open the rest of the way. Before she could even think of anything to say her friend was gone and she was standing alone like a lost sheep. Resolutely she pulled herself together, tucked her books under one arm and headed down the corridor to Mr. Chalmers' classroom. She got there just in time, nodded quickly to a few friends whom she hadn't seen since June, and sank gratefully into a seat in the second row, trying to turn her attention to the undeniably fascinating topic of intermediate algebra.

Her mind refused to obey. Time and time again her attention wandered and she found herself spending the bulk of the period thinking about what Bonnie had told her, wondering whether her friend had been kidding her or telling the truth. It seemed impossible, but Bonnie certainly hadn't sounded as though she was kidding.

Bonnie's second-hour class was not intermediate algebra.

It was English with Miss Muriel Lynch, and as Bonnie listened to Miss Lynch expound to great length upon the delights of a vacation in New Hampshire, she amused herself by trying to imagine the dried-up old bag getting initiated into the Unicorns. The mental picture she got was so hysterical she had trouble controlling the laughter that welled up within her. Imagine old lady Lynch flat on her back with her knees pointing at the sky!

It just couldn't happen, Bonnie decided. Scrawny old Lynch was one of those freaks who wouldn't know what to do with a man if she came home one night and found one lying in her bed with his pants down.

Scrawny old Lynch. She'd probably look between his legs and not know what the thing there was for. Maybe the old battle-axe would try to pick her nose with it.

At this point Bonnie giggled. Miss Lynch frowned tolerantly at the girl and went on talking and Bonnie managed to suppress the giggle. But it was so funny! The idea of the old biddy picking her nose . . .

Bonnie wouldn't pick her nose, that was for sure. Even before she joined the Unicorns and found out what everything was all about, even then she had known quite a lot about the whole thing. She had known how babies were created and how they were prevented, and while some of the mechanics of the sex act were naturally out of the realm of her knowledge, she had a pretty good idea what two people did when they found themselves in bed together.

But what she had known then was nothing to what she knew now. Now, she thought, in her own small way she was an expert. Not that there wasn't a lot she still had to learn. Not that there wasn't a lot she was going to learn, for that matter. But now she knew what to do and how to do it—more important, she knew what it felt like.

And it felt wonderful.

Oh, she had expected that much before. She and Chuck hadn't exactly been strangers while they were going together. He had a car—that is, he had the privilege of borrowing his father's Pontiac when they went out together. And a car made matters much simpler. A car was a private little bedroom on wheels and this was very nice indeed.

But she and Chuck had never gone all the way, at least not while school was in session. He had wanted to, that was for sure. So had she, for that matter. And the two of them certainly didn't try to keep their distance from each other. But somehow it had never quite happened, perhaps because she had never permitted it and perhaps because he had never quite insisted upon it. They had, in the contemporary idiom, "done everything else but."

Their relationship followed the usual pattern. On the first date Chuck kissed her at the door. As time passed the kisses were longer and more intense. When they started going steady they went in for long kissing sessions in which the full possibilities of the kiss were explored. No more pecking with the lips tight together—that was juvenile. Instead their mouths opened and their tongues met and did things and the individual kisses often lasted for five minutes or more. It had taken her a couple tries before she discovered how to kiss and breathe at the same time, but she was a fast study.

The kissing made her feel funny. Later on when he touched her breast through her sweater for the first time that made her feel funny too in much the same way. Her breasts were small but very firm and very sensitive and she liked the way her nipples got all stiff and funny when he touched her there. Evidently he liked the whole thing himself, for the two of them would spend hours sitting together, his hands manipulating her breasts, his mouth glued to hers, the Pontiac parked in a dark lane on the outskirts of the town.

Progress. There was the time when he wanted to unhook her bra and she wouldn't let him. There was the time, on their next date a night later, when she did let him unhook her bra and his hands on her bare breasts drove her wild. It was much better without clothing in the way, much better indeed. All the sensations were intensified and the pleasure was increased proportionately.

Progress.

And more progress.

There was the time when he put his hand on her knee, then moved it up to her thigh. It felt good, but when he looked at her questioningly she shook her head and he stopped.

The next time she didn't shake her head and he didn't stop.

No one had ever touched her there before. She had touched herself—all girls did, she was privately certain—but it was hardly the same thing. She could feel his fingers very clearly through the sheer white silk of her panties and they brought her a degree of excitement that no form of petting had ever brought her before. Neither of them wanted to stop that night.

But they did.

Progress.

The next time they went out she was very cute about the whole thing. She didn't wear anything under her skirt that night and he let out a little gasp of shock mingled with pleasure when his searching fingers found no obstacles between themselves and the object they sought. His pleasure was more than equaled by her own. She writhed on the back seat of the car, her breath sounding unreal in her ears, her whole body twisting in a passion that was agony to suppress.

But they "controlled themselves" that night. It was spring, April, but they managed to control themselves for the remainder of the school year. Fear of pregnancy or fear of discovery, it was perhaps more a feeling they shared that intercourse was wrong that kept them from giving in to their passions.

They were clever kids. They discovered that if he handled her in a certain manner she could experience an orgasm and consequently could relax. The release she gained that way was nothing in comparison to the release derived from intercourse, but she did not know this at the time and was grateful for whatever release she could get.

Similarly, he showed her what she should do to give him the same sort of pleasure. At first she didn't enjoy touching him but it seemed only fair to bring him an equivalent sort of fulfillment, and in time she grew to enjoy the caress, enjoy having him firm and demanding in her hands, enjoy the excitement that coursed through him and the pleasure that her hands brought to him.

If it hadn't been for Dean Hanson they might have gone on that way until they both graduated from high school and were married. Chuck's father owned a small grocery store and Chuck would go into business. They would marry, rent an apartment, then buy a house as soon as they could afford it. Bonnie might well have remained a virgin until her wedding night when a license from the Commonwealth of Massachusetts would certify that she and Chuck were duly authorized to copulate to their mutual satisfaction.

Instead they met Dean Hanson.

That changed things.

Dean Hanson was an adolescent the same as Bonnie and Chuck and Ed and Mary. The only tangible difference between him and them was that they were seventeen or eighteen and he was twenty-six. At least one man like Hanson is as much a requirement of a town like Palmer as the village square and the town drunk.

Hanson's parents were no longer living. While they lived they had been wealthy, wealthy enough so that there had never been and would never be any reason for Hanson to go to work. Hanson, who certainly would not work if he didn't have to and probably wouldn't have worked even if it was absolutely necessary, lived by himself in the house on State Street where he had been born. Each year his friends were a small group of high school seniors. When they graduated he made friends with the succeeding batch of seniors, and the years passed in this fashion.

This particular year, however, Hanson succeeded in accomplishing something which had been the sole ambition of a generally ambitionless life.

He organized the Unicorns.

Besides Hanson himself, six girls and five boys were the charter members of the Unicorns. They met once a week in the basement of Hanson's large house where they conducted the affairs of the meeting in complete and total privacy. This was fortunate, for the other residents of State Street would have been more than a little surprised and more than a little taken aback by the goings-on at the meetings of the Unicorns.

The Unicorns had orgies.

The club began simply enough. The twelve of them met, watched a pornographic movie which Hanson obtained from a dealer in Boston who specialized in that sort of thing, paired off and withdrew to individual rooms where they had intercourse. This was just a beginning.

As time went by the program of the meetings became a bit more elaborate. The sexual activities were stepped up and became more complicated. The private aspect of intercourse in individual rooms changed to mass sex scenes.

The six girls in the Unicorns were Betty Jo Meltzer, Anne Kessler, Judy Simmons, Ruthellen Perkins, Gladys Kent and Lesley Banks. The five boys were Marv Gardens, Jack Lacey, Alan Marshall, Dave Carson and Larry Prince.

On the first of July they added two new members. The two new members were Chuck Folsom and Bonnie Leigh.

Remembering, Bonnie couldn't be sure just how she and Chuck had decided to join the club. It had been Chuck's idea but she hadn't offered any tremendous resistance to the whole idea. Probably the underlying reason why both of them were eager enough to be members was that it would give them a chance to go all the way without feeling guilty about it. If they did so on their own it was something secret, solitary, and therefore shameful. While the acts themselves might be "worse" on the crowd level, the necessary sense of group participation would be present to ease the feelings of guilt. If everybody also was doing it, then it wasn't so bad after all, was it?

The initiation hadn't been fun at first. The movie was nice, of course—it was interesting to Bonnie because, as vivid as her imagination had been, she hadn't completely understood the sex act as she did after she saw it performed in full detail by images on a movie screen. It was exciting as well as interesting, and when hands began to fondle her while she watched she found herself getting all hot and excited.

Then the movie was over and the initiation began.

The price of membership was that she submit to every boy in the club, starting with Hanson. This bothered her a little; it seemed to her only fitting that her first lover be Chuck. But the rules were the rules, and since Hanson was the leader of the club she supposed it was only right that he go first.

It hurt when he did it to her but not as much as she thought it would. He was finished before she was really excited, but then another boy took his place, and another took his, and so on until each and every one of them had made love to her. By the time they had finished she was, in the language of the trade, "broken to saddle." She watched happily while Chuck went through his initiation and then they were both members of the club.

She didn't envy Mary her summer at camp. If Mary had any idea of what she was missing she would flip, Bonnie thought to herself. Meetings every Thursday, and that one great meeting when they initiated Laura Rose and Ray Saltonstall.

Meetings once a week, with each meeting better than the last. And on top of that she and Chuck didn't have to hold themselves in any more. He was still her steady—whatever happened in Hanson's basement was just part of the club. And their dates now concluded in a much more satisfying manner, with the two of them making love with no holds barred.

Poor Mary. Well, if Mary and Ed were game, their turn would come soon enough. Mary was shocked, but any girl would be shocked at first. She would talk to her at lunch and get her interested, and if Al Marshall managed to get Ed equally interested they might have two more members to initiate the following night.

That would be something, she thought. She looked up at Miss Lynch and smiled a secretive smile to herself. *You old bitch*, she thought. *You wouldn't know what to do if you had a man between your legs. But I would. I'd know just what to do and I'd love every minute of it. I'd squirm all over the place and drive him crazy.*

Yes, she decided, she had to get Ed and Mary into the club. It was funny—usually the girls were more afraid of the idea of the Unicorns than the boys were. Just the idea of having as much sex as anybody could possibly want was usually enough to make a boy forget whatever scruples he might have had about the whole thing.

But she had a feeling it wasn't going to be that way with Ed. He was sort of . . . well, not exactly straight-laced, but damned close to it. He'd probably be dead set against the whole thing, and it would probably be Mary who'd get excited about the idea first. Well, it figured that Mary would be a natural for the club. A girl with a body like that couldn't let it go to waste. And the boys in the club were sure hot to get a little of Mary. Hanson had told her that if there was one girl in the world he wanted a piece of, Mary was the girl. Bonnie could understand why.

But Ed—well, Bonnie wouldn't mind having some of Ed herself. It would be interesting to see what he was like. He'd probably be all goofy and shy at first, but she was willing to lay odds that he'd be damned good once he got used to it. He was a good-looking guy, and he sure had a good build on him. What she'd seen of him, anyway. And she was certain that what she hadn't seen was just as nice.

When the bell rang she hardly realized it, and she hauled herself out of her seat realizing that she sat through the entire class without listening to a thing old Lynch had said. She stopped one of the boys to ask him if there had been an assignment and was happy to learn that there hadn't. Then she hurried on down the hall to her next class. It wasn't a class, really just a study hall, but it would give her a chance to sit and think about what she was going to tell Mary without some dried-up hag like Lynch babbling at her.

It was a bad day for listening to teachers. Ed Bainbridge was trying to listen to Mrs. Seidenberg's biology lecture but he couldn't keep his mind on what she was saying. He was too burned-up inside to think straight.

God, he was mad! Al Marshall had always been something of a snake, but he couldn't believe the jerk would suggest something like what he suggested. He only hinted at it but Ed knew what he was getting at and he sure as hell didn't want any part of it.

A sex club, for God's sake!

Real cute. It was bad enough if those fool kids wanted to put themselves through hell, but he sure as hell wasn't going to take a trip to hell along with them. The nerve of them to expect him and Mary to go for a crazy bit like that! Not him—if the time ever came when he needed something like that he would go have his head examined. And certainly not Mary—she was a good girl, a clean girl, a decent girl. He and Mary necked a little sure, that was only normal and there would have been something wrong with them if they didn't. But as far as anything else went they could damn well wait until they were married. Doing it ahead of time was like opening your Christmas presents in midsummer. Fun then, but it loused up your Christmas for you.

He sat in his seat and simmered. Somebody ought to expose the whole damn thing, he thought. Well, it would come to light eventually. And then the bunch of them would get what they had coming. As far as he was concerned, he and Mary would keep clear from the whole bunch. Let them have their fun, if that was what they called it.

CHAPTER 2

George McCauley Trevelyn, one of too few historians who have failed to treat English as a dead language, made a rather interesting observation in admonishing those history scholars who approach history as an exact science. History can never be as scientific as the laboratory sciences, he reasoned, if only because it is impossible to test the validity of any hypothesis. No control pattern can be established and no experiment can be repeated.

By the same token, one cannot say with assurance that the lives of sixteen students at Nathan Palmer High School would have turned out in a graphically different manner if Coach Fred Lagniappe had not chosen to ignore the contents of Marv "Moose" Gardens' locker.

"That's how it's shaping up," Lagniappe told the football squad at the organizational meeting that afternoon. "We're strong on the line and weak in the backfield. We ought to be pretty light on our passing attack, fair to middling on the ground and tight as a vise on defense."

The team nodded stupidly.

"You guys have a lot of potential," he went on. "Middleburgh will be tough and Litchfield'll be tougher—they won the valley championship last year and they've got most of their first string back. A few more teams can make it close and the rest of the schedule ought to be pushovers. But that's only if you guys pitch in and work. You gotta make it as a team or you'll get knocked on your asses by everybody from Squeedunk Central to East Plainfield Nursing Academy."

This is not all Lagniappe had to say, but for the sake of brevity we can forget the rest of his remarks. He talked, and he talked, and he talked. Perhaps this was a waste of breath: more likely it made good sense to say everything three times to the dolts on the football squad in the vague hope that some of it might sink in. But for our purposes it should be sufficient to say that eventually he ran out of talk and the team left the locker room, leaving Coach Lagniappe the task of cleaning up and getting the hell home to his wife.

After the team filed out of the room Fred Lagniappe sat down on a grey wooden bench and rested his head in his hands and his elbows on his thighs. It was a comfortable position and Fred Lagniappe was a comfortable man. A high school hero himself, he had been good enough to get a football scholarship to Northwestern and not good enough to wind up playing pro ball. As a result he finished college and went to work doing what he had always wanted to do—coaching his own high school's football, basketball and baseball teams.

It was a good life. It was basically a simple job and the life he led was hardly complex—a small three-bedroom white frame house on Whitmore Street. A wife who loved him, a kid who thought that, if he wasn't God, he was easily the next best thing.

The coach stood up, flexed muscles that were still supple although, as he kept reminding himself, his jockstrap days were over, made a quick show of straightening the locker room and headed for the door. On the way out he noticed that one of the football players had left his locker ajar and he started to close it. Something made him glance inside the locker—maybe he wanted to know whose locker it was so that he could remind the boy to keep it securely shut in the future. But what he found stopped him cold.

Fred Lagniappe took the sheaf of 5x7 photos from the locker and studied them. The photos were professionally taken and professionally finished, and a photographer would no doubt have taken a certain amount of interest in the lighting tricks and angles employed by whoever took the pictures. But Lagniappe didn't bother with camera angles or lighting tricks. He was more interested in the subject matter.

The photos were what is known in the pornography business as "action shots." Unlike the nude figure studies and near-nude pin-ups which are peddled on more or less open market, action shots involve more than one person engaging in some sexual activity or other. They range in complexity from trite shots of the more commonplace sexual positions to bizarre mob scenes embracing several sexual aberrations.

Moose Gardens had an extremely imaginative set in his locker.

The first three pictures showed a man and a woman in three variant positions of intercourse. The woman was a funny-faced blonde with generous breasts and a well-formed rear end. The man was short and swarthy. He had a ghoulish grin on his fat face in two of the three pictures; his face was turned away from the camera in the third.

The rest of the set were more involved. Several of them included children having sex with adults. In still another one a dog and a woman were the featured performers. The variety was so great and the photography so excellent from a technical point of view that Coach Lagniappe, who had been around a bit in his not-too-distant youth, realized at once that this was not the average adolescent's collection of pornography.

Lagniappe glanced into the locker to see if there were any more pictures around. There weren't, but what he did find was even more provocative. He found a box of one dozen contraceptives. The box had been broken and three of the condoms were missing.

Now what in the world was the best tackle on the squad doing with nine condoms and a few dozen action shots?

Lagniappe scratched his head and wrinkled up his face into a simian grimace. Something was wrong here; something was going on and he didn't much like it. Hell, every kid in high school bought a rubber sometime and carried it around with him with the devotion of a mendicant. Fred Lagniappe had done it himself, just as he had owned a small store of pornography. But, God damn it, he sure as hell never bought the things by the dozen when he was in high school. He got his nookie, everybody got his nookie, but not so frequently that he needed a dozen of the damn things all at once.

And the pictures! The coach took them out again and gave them a quick run-through. One particular shot of a boy about twelve years old with two women in their thirties made him sick to his stomach. To think there were people who would pose for pictures like that! It was enough to make you puke green.

Not to mention the fact that they had to shanghai a twelve-year-old kid into it. Being a pervert yourself was bad enough,

Lagniappe figured, but at least it was your own business. When you had to louse up kids who didn't know any better it was time for them to take you out and blow your head off.

Fred Lagniappe's first impulse was to inform the school authorities. He had a gnawing feeling that something was wrong, something he should open up about. But that might get Moose in trouble, he realized, and Moose was one hell of a nice kid. He also was the best tackle on the squad and a close contender for best tackle in the state outside of that truckhorse of a kid from Boston Central, and without him any dreams of the valley flag were so much nonsense.

No, he decided, there was no sense getting the kid in trouble. What the hell difference did it make if the kid liked to knock off a piece now and then? Hell, kids were getting freer with it every minute; there were fifteen– and sixteen-year-old girls walking around who looked as though they were dying for it. Why should Moose get hell just because he was sharp enough to be getting his tail? Why knock him out of the running for a good scholarship to a good school?

As far as the pictures went, nobody ever got into trouble looking at pictures. If Moose was so damned good with the girls, maybe he liked to show them pictures to get them hot. Hell, that could be. And it was the kid's business anyway. Hell, he wasn't hurting anybody. To hell with the pictures.

Coach Lagniappe felt better instantly. He was, as has been said, an uncomplicated man. He hated decisions; when he had to make them he made up his mind quickly, once and for all. Then he could put the whole problem out of his mind, say a quick to hell with it and think about more important things.

He forgot all about Moose's locker and its contents the minute he had replaced the pictures and the condoms and had locked the locker securely.

But he didn't forget the one picture, the disgusting one showing the sickening things those two women were doing to that little kid. He couldn't forget it. He remembered it all the way home to the white frame house on Whitmore Street where he braked the car to a sudden stop, raced inside, grabbed his wife, kissed her passionately and hustled her off to the bedroom as fast as he possibly could. While they made love his eyes were shut tight and his brain was filled to overflowing with the terrifying image of the young boy and the two women and the nauseating stomach-churning things they were doing.

It was just one of those nights, Mary decided. Just one of those nights when things weren't working out right at all. She and Ed were sitting across from each other in a booth at the Clip Clop Soda Mill and the table that separated them might just as well have been an ocean. They were that far apart.

It was worse than that. Here they were, sitting close enough and sipping identical cokes, and they just weren't talking to each other the way they usually did. He wanted to talk. She could tell by the way he was acting that there was something on his mind and it wasn't hard for her to guess what it was.

If Bonnie had devoted her entire lunch hour to explaining the club to her, it seemed more than likely that Ed had heard the same general story from one of the male members of the organization. Obviously it was on his mind, obviously he wanted to talk about it, and just as obviously he had studiously avoided bringing it up without managing to get it off his mind. They hadn't needed to come to the Soda Mill. They could have spent the evening in her living room the way they usually did when he came over to her house during the week. They would sit and watch television with her parents and her brother Jimmy until her parents and Jimmy went upstairs to leave them alone. Then they could kiss a little and talk a little in complete privacy.

But instead he had brought her to the Soda Mill, where there was no privacy to speak of, and that meant that he wanted to talk to her but was afraid to broach the subject. Well, she could understand it. It was hardly the sort of thing they usually talked about. In fact if there was any fault she could find with Ed it was that he was . . . well, maybe a little too prudish with her. He could be a little more open, a little less inclined to play the role of the rock-bound New England Puritan with her.

A disturbing thought came to her. Maybe, just maybe, Ed wanted to join the club. He didn't seem to be the type who would want something like that, but she couldn't be sure about it. She knew that men were supposed to want as many women as they could have, but how could a boy like Ed be willing to share her with other boys? Not Ed, she decided firmly. If anything he was over-possessive. He couldn't let anybody else near her.

She finished her coke, making noises with the straw when she hit the bottom of the glass. "Let's get out of here," she said, and he nodded and finished his own coke in a hurry and left two dimes on the Formica tabletop. Her hand found his and they walked out of the Soda Mill and out onto the street.

"Ed?"

He looked at her.

"Bonnie told me about the club, honey."

He let out his breath and seemed to relax. "That's what I wanted to talk about. I didn't know whether she did or not and I didn't know how to bring it up."

"Well, she did."

"I figured she would. I heard she was mixed up in this mess and I figured she'd want to get you in on it."

The tone of his voice told her how far off she had been in speculating that he might want to join the club. He sounded as though he wanted to draw and quarter everybody who was in it or something.

"What did you want to talk about?"

He shrugged. "I don't know. I just wanted to say what a filthy thing it is."

"It sure is."

"You read about those things," he said. "But who would figure it for our high school and with people we know?"

"Like Bonnie. She's my best friend."

"She was your best friend. I don't see how you can be friendly with her now."

She didn't have any answer for this. She didn't want to tell him that she still felt close to Bonnie, that she couldn't cut an emotion off just like that. So she didn't say anything in answer.

"I'll tell you something," he went on. "I think we ought to tell somebody."

"What do you mean?"

"Tell somebody," he repeated. "About the club they've got and what they're doing."

"You mean tattle-tale?"

His lips curled. "That's a pretty babyish word for it, isn't it?"

"You know what I mean."

"It's not a matter of . . . tattling," he said doggedly. "Those kids are going to get into an awful lot of trouble. They'll wind up being perverted for the rest of their lives with what they're doing."

"It's their business."

He stared at her. "Do you mean that?"

"Why shouldn't I?"

"How old are they, Mary? Seventeen and eighteen? Is it their business if they wreck their lives for good?"

She frowned impatiently. "I think you're making a federal case out of it. It's not a matter of ruining their lives, Ed. They're just playing around. They're kids like we are and they're fooling around."

"*Fooling around!*"

She fell silent.

"Fooling around," he repeated. "Mary, it's not just a matter of necking parties or anything like that. This is serious. They're having intercourse."

"I know."

"And I say it's terrible."

"And I say whatever they do is up to them."

She barely recognized his expression when he looked at her. "You know," he said, "I'd almost guess you half-want to join in the fun."

"Ed!"

"Sure," he said, his voice mean, "I can just picture you now lying on your back with one of those guys on top of you and—"

"Don't talk to me like that!"

He broke off at once and the shame showed on his face. Turning her by the shoulders he took her in his arms and held her close to him. "Honey," he said, his voice softer and gentler now. "Honey, you know I didn't mean it. You know that."

She couldn't say anything and she felt tears welling up behind her eyes.

"You know it, Mary. It's just that I can't be with you and think about filth like that at the same time. It's horrible. And you're clean, perfectly clean, and the way I feel about you is clean, and—"

She broke the embrace, took his hand in hers and gave it a squeeze. "I understand," she said thinly. "Don't talk about it any more. Everything's all right."

They walked to her house in silence. It was only a few minutes after nine but the sky was dark already, reminding her that summer was over and fall had taken its place. The sky was moonless and starless and the streets of Palmer at that hour were deserted and silent. She felt suddenly very much alone and even the fact that Ed was holding her hand did not thoroughly dispel the feeling. There was something positively ominous about the night and the darkness and the mood that had come over her. She tried to shake herself free of the mood, tried to push aside the feeling of aloneness by holding his hand tighter and taking reassurance from the answering pressure of his fingers on her moist palm, but this did little good and the feeling persisted.

Her house was a trim recently-painted frame house on Avondale Road with a lush green lawn in front and in the back yard as well. A flagstone path led from the sidewalk to the front door and they walked along the path hand in hand, still not saying a word.

The door was open—the Hobsons never locked their doors, believing firmly that one of the advantages of a tiny town like Palmer was the relative immunity from burglaries.

She opened the door and stood awkwardly on the threshold. The downstairs was dark and she knew that her parents and Jimmy were upstairs and probably asleep. They all went to bed early; it was rare to find anybody awake after nine-thirty and quite often they were all sacked out before nine.

"Ed?"

He shifted from one foot to the other.

"Will you come in for awhile?"

He hesitated.

"They're asleep," she put in quickly. "I wish you'd come in. Just for a few minutes."

He smiled and stepped into the hallway and she closed the door. He led the way into the living room and was reaching for the knob on the television set when her voice stopped him.

"Leave it off, Ed. I just want you to sit next to me for awhile."

He nodded obediently and took a seat beside her on the love seat. For a moment or so neither of them said a word or made a move and she couldn't take it. She reached for him and he took her into his arms and all at once their mouths were together and they were kissing.

It was an eminently proper kiss—too proper, as far as Mary was concerned. She wanted his tongue in her mouth and his arms as tight around her as bands of steel. But even with their mouths closed the kiss lasted a long time and she was more composed by the time it ended.

"I . . . needed that," she said.

He nodded.

"Kiss me again, Ed."

He kissed her again and this time the kiss was more what she had in mind. It was she who took the initiative, she who parted his lips with her eager tongue and she who caressed his tongue in turn. But he wasn't exactly left out in the cold. She felt his pulse quicken as she kissed him and as he responded to the kiss and returned it in full.

The kiss ended and was replaced seconds later by another kiss. Sitting in his arms, kissing him and receiving his kisses, she knew exactly what would happen from then until he would leave her house. They would continue to kiss, the kisses would become more passionate, he would take her face in his hands and kiss her eyes and cheeks and ears, and finally, as a cap to the evening's love match, his hands would caress her breasts through their chaste protective covering of blouse and bra. This would continue for awhile, then they would taper off with kisses and then he would go.

And that would be that.

Suddenly she resented it, resented that she knew every move he would make far in advance, resented in fact that he always stopped without being asked to stop. For one thing, a little kissing and breast handling certainly didn't satisfy her. It just about got her excited and ready for more and then it was time for them to stop. And, because this was repeated in just the same manner every time they were alone together like this, each time the small amount of kissing and touching left her a little more aroused and, paradoxically, a little further from satisfaction.

Moreover, she was annoyed that he was the one who exerted

absolute control over himself, that it was he who decided how far to go and when to stop. Even if she wouldn't let him go any further—and this seemed doubtful right about then—still it would make her feel a lot better if she had to *tell* him to stop.

This way she felt almost . . . well, cheap. As if he took care that nothing would happen while she was too passionate to call the shots. She didn't like it at all.

The necking session followed its inevitable course except that this night she got a little more excited than usual. Perhaps it was the talks with Bonnie about the sex club and the whole idea of having intercourse with boys. Then again it may have been that it had been awhile since she and Ed had been alone together this way. Whatever it was her kisses were fiercer and more intense than usual, and when his hand held her breast she covered it with her own hand and pressed him to her almost savagely.

Then, seconds later, he was withdrawing his hand and pushing her away gently and the inevitable letdown that came with thwarted passion enveloped her like a soggy blanket of woolly ashes.

"Whew! We'd better watch ourselves, honey."

She nodded automatically.

"We can't let ourselves get out of control."

She started to nod again but something deep within her made her stifle the nod and answer by placing his hand on her breast again. The suddenness of her act caught him by surprise and his lips came down on hers like a hawk on a chicken. His hand tightened on her warm flesh and his tongue buried itself in the sweetness of her mouth.

But only for a minute. Then it was over and he had shifted imperceptibly away from her on the seat.

"I better get going now," he said, adding unnecessarily, "before something happens."

She didn't trust herself to speak. She stood up and walked to the door with him but she didn't hold his hand on the way. She was afraid that if she touched him just then she would be unable to restrain herself from embracing him once more, and although at this point she was only too aware of his annoying ability to control himself just like Emily Post's little boy, she didn't want him to think that she was nothing but a little slut.

He opened the door and stepped halfway through it—more of the ritual—and reached out his arms for her. This time the goodnight kiss was nothing but a swift peck on the lips followed by that soft smile of his and a whispered *See you tomorrow*.

Then he was gone.

CHAPTER 3

She supposed that she ought to do her homework but she honestly didn't feel like it, not just then. She wasn't sure what she felt like doing, just what she did not feel like doing. She didn't feel like watching television and she didn't feel like reading and she most definitely didn't feel like talking to anybody.

She walked back to the living room, sat down in a red armchair and closed her eyes. It was pitch-dark in there even with her eyes opened but she felt like keeping them closed to shut out the world. Her head was spinning a little and her cheeks were flushed and her breasts fairly ached with suppressed desire.

What was the matter with Ed, anyway? Didn't he want her the same way that she wanted him? He said he did, but maybe he was just talking through his hat. Maybe he didn't feel things as deeply as she did.

Because she certainly did feel things deeply. Not that she wanted to go all the way—that might be a little more than she was ready for. But this we-have-to-wait-until-we're-married stuff coupled with the-less-we-do-the-easier-it'll-be-to-control-ourselves stuff wasn't giving her what she wanted and needed.

Control. That was Ed's magic word. He was so darned controlled it was a wonder he managed to move a muscle. He was a robot, that's what he was, and if he cared so much for her as he said he did it was a wonder he couldn't show it more in his actions instead of just talking about it and leaving her so shook up.

And the way he got so wrought up about the sex club. Well, as far as she was concerned it was their business what they did and not his. Maybe they had the right idea. At least they weren't going through what she was going through. They were having their fun and using their bodies unencumbered by that magic word *control*.

Control.

After a few minutes she went into the breakfast nook and got to work on her homework. That was where she liked to do her studying—it was quieter and cooler down there and she could work without fear of disturbing the rest of the family. Besides, that way she was right by the downstairs phone in case anybody called her and she could pick it up as soon as it rang before anybody else heard it and woke up.

There wasn't much in the way of homework. Just the usual beginning-of-the-year round of introductory assignments and she whipped through them easily. She was just finishing the last of the algebra problems when the phone rang. It was Bonnie.

"Hi," she said. "Remember what we were talking about at lunch?"

"I remember."

"Well, we're having a meeting tomorrow night and we'd like you to come and see what it's like."

Earlier she would have simply refused and that would have been that. But now something made her say: "Ed doesn't like the idea."

"How about you?"

"I—"

"Mary, we figured Ed wouldn't go for it. He's a little . . . well, stuffy, wouldn't you say?"

"I guess so," she said, not defending him as she would normally have done. Because he was stuffy. And reserved and cold.

"Look, Mary. Why don't you come down alone? Don't tell him about it. Just come down and see what it's like. If you don't go for it at least you'll have a chance to see what it's all about."

"Oh, I couldn't."

"You don't have to *do* anything, honey. We're having special movies and everything. I think you might learn something."

"I . . . what kind of movies?"

"Interesting ones. Let's leave it at that. I think you'll find them interesting—unless you're scared. You aren't are you?"

"Of course not. But—"

"Then why not come? To hell with Ed."

Yes, she thought angrily. *To hell with Ed.*

"What time?"

"Eight-thirty," Bonnie told her. "You know where Dean's house is?"

She knew Hanson's house.

"I'll probably see you in school," Bonnie said. "If I don't, I'll see you at the meeting."

Chapter 4

John Schwerner leaned back in his chair behind the ancient oak desk in Room 312. Then in a quick movement he half-threw himself forward so that his elbows rested upon the desk blotter and his eyes peered alertly into the eyes of the boy standing in front of his desk.

"I'm glad you came in to see me, Ed. Why don't you pull up a chair? The only students who have to stand while I sit are the ones who throw spitballs at me. Go ahead sit down."

Ed Bainbridge smiled and sat down. That, he thought, was the great thing about Mr. Schwerner. He talked to you like one person to another. There was never anything stuffy about him. This, coupled with the fact that he was the best lecturer and fairest marker in the school, made him a tremendous asset to the faculty of Nathan Palmer High.

"Well," Schwerner said. "They way I get it, you want to be a lawyer. That how it looks to you?"

Ed nodded.

"Why?"

He thought for a few seconds. "I don't know exactly," he admitted. "It's just that it's more interesting to me than anything else."

"Know anything about what it's like to practice law?"

"A little."

"Like what?"

"Well, I've done quite a bit of reading. The reading I like to do seems to fit in with law."

"Don't tell me you've been reading law books!"

Ed grinned. "Nothing that deep, I'm afraid. Mostly biographies of criminal lawyers."

"Like who?"

"Fallon and Darrow and Rogers and Leibowitz."

Schwerner nodded approvingly. "Great men," he said. "Fallon was probably something of a crook and Rogers was probably something of a drunkard while Darrow and Leibowitz were two of the finest men this country ever saw. But the four of them were top lawyers, top lawyers."

Ed fell silent.

"Well," Schwerner went on, "that's an important interest. What I find even more encouraging is that the subjects you're interested in are the ones you'll have to concentrate on in a pre-law course. History is your favorite course, isn't it? Or have you been brown-nosing me?"

"Probably both."

Schwerner laughed. "Good answer. I don't think there's any problem, Ed. History's an ideal pre-law major and with your grades you can land a top scholarship to a good school with no trouble at all. And the fact that you're a white Anglo-Saxon Protestant certainly won't work to your disadvantage. What did you want to talk to me about?"

"I'm trying to settle on a college."

"What do your folks have to say about it?"

"They're pushing for an Ivy League school, preferably Harvard or Yale. But they'll let me go wherever I want to go."

"I see. Well, there are advantages in Harvard and Yale. I think you'd probably prefer Princeton personally if you did decide on one of the Big Three, but with any of them there's a big prestige advantage. You stand a better chance of getting into a prestige law school from a prestige college, and from a prestige law school you have a much easier time of ending up in a top-drawer firm. If that's what you're looking for."

"It isn't."

Schwerner grinned. "Don't be too sure of it. Right now you're keen on criminal law—in a few years you might want to settle for the security of a good position with a good firm. Criminal law doesn't make many people rich."

"I know."

Schwerner glanced at his watch, then turned back to Ed. "Personally," he said, "I think you'd lose a lot of your potential at Harvard or Yale or even Princeton. They're pretty narrow places in a lot of respects. I'd rather see you in one of the good small schools. Swarthmore, say or Reed or Carleton or Antioch or Middlebury or Clifton. I went to Clifton myself but don't let that sway you for or against the place. Why don't you write for catalogues from the six I mentioned and see how they strike you? You've got time before you have to start applying and you might as well put it to good use. After you've rummaged through the catalogues come on back and we'll talk it over."

"I'll do that," Ed said. He finished jotting down the six colleges Schwerner had mentioned and capped his pen. "Thanks very much," he said, rising. "I'd better get back to my study hall before Miss Merriman starts wondering where I am."

Schwerner nodded, then scribbled something on a slip of paper. "Here," he said. "This'll let her know where you were." Ed took the slip and Schwerner asked: "There wasn't anything else on your mind, was there?"

Ed hesitated. If there was anyone in the school he could talk to about the Unicorns, Schwerner was the one. But maybe Mary had a point—maybe he should mind his own business.

"No," he said. "That's all."

Dean Hanson's residence was the second-best house on State Street. Second only to the Comstock Mansion in size and elegance, it cast an impressive shadow both figuratively and literally. The comparative worth of the Hanson family, however, was not commensurate with the comparative worth of the Hanson House. It had been built years and years ago when the Hansons were one of the leading families in town. Now Dean was the only Hanson left in the town, and while the house would be his as long as he lived, any social position that had been left to him had long since vanished.

Hanson took the cigarette stub from his ivory-and-ebony holder and stubbed it out in a black ashtray, a huge bowl which had been carved from a single piece of obsidian. He fitted another cigarette into the holder and lit it with a rather vulgar cigarette lighter carved to resemble a naked African female of rather astounding proportions. The mechanism of the lighter was triggered by flipping a lever between the woman's breasts, thus causing a jet of flame to shoot out from between her full thighs.

"Then it's set," he said to Bonnie Leigh. "Tonight at eight the full membership will assemble here in the basement as usual. At eight-thirty Mary will arrive and the program will start."

"That's right."

Hanson nodded. "Everybody has been informed of the meeting? You've taken care of that?"

"It's all set," she said. She passed her tongue over her lips and looked at Hanson. He was tall and strikingly thin, with jet black hair that was so long it was almost effeminate and slender fingers that heightened the impression. But she knew there was nothing queer about him—he had proved that to her quite successfully. Remembering the times she had done it with him caused a tremor of excitement to run through her and she rubbed her thighs together involuntarily like a cricket rubbing its hind legs to make music.

"This boy of hers," Hanson was saying. "This Ed something-or-other."

"Bainbridge."

"Bainbridge," he repeated. "As I understand it, he knows nothing about the meeting. He was told about the club. And Mary said he'd never go for it, that it seemed best to invite the girl but to leave him out of it. That's right isn't it?"

"That's right. I wish we could get him to join but he's pretty square that way. Al told me he flew off the handle and flipped completely when he heard about the club. And Mary said he'd never go for it."

"But she will."

Bonnie considered. "Not exactly. She doesn't want to join or anything, at least not right now. I told her not to say anything to Ed but just to come along to the meeting tonight to find out what it's like. I told her there'd be a movie and all."

"Fine," said Hanson. He deposited the ash from his cigarette in the obsidian ashtray and smiled to himself. "Fine," he repeated.

"What's the movie going to be like?"

"You'll like it," he assured her. "It's somewhat different from the others."

She moistened her lips and a feeling of excitement caught her up. "Tell me about it."

He held out his hands palm upward. "Nothing to tell," he said. "You'll see for yourself. But there's one important difference."

"What's that?"

"It's in color. Not black-and-white like the others but full color."

The thought alone of the movie they would see that night acted as a sexual stimulant and Bonnie didn't want to sit in the chair by herself any longer. She got up and went to Hanson, sitting in his lap and putting her arms around him.

"That sounds good," she said.

"It is good. I only wish it were accompanied by a sound track. I think it would be pleasant to listen to them moaning and squealing while they were doing it."

Bonnie took a deep breath and snuggled closer to Hanson. Her small firm breasts pressed into his chest and she liked the familiar feel of his body against hers.

"Dean," she murmured huskily. She reached out a hand and ran it through his long hair. "Dean . . ."

He laughed softly. "Careful," he said. "The school thinks you went home because you were sick. It wouldn't be proper to leave school for the worthy purpose of making love, would it?"

"To hell with the school," she said. She pressed closer to him and caressed his throat with her fingertips.

"Besides," he went on, "I have to conserve my energy for the Girl of the Luscious Breasts, the lovely Miss Mary Hobson. So you don't want to tire me out in advance."

"She's just coming to watch, Dean."

He smiled tolerantly. "Of course she is," he said. "But if she decides that she's interested in more than a voyeuristic role, who are we to deny her the pleasure of participating in our more active pursuits? It is, needless to say, up to the young girl with the fabulous breasts to choose."

"Oh," she said. "I get it. You mean rape."

He frowned. "Bonnie, Bonnie, Bonnie. You have such a coarse outlook at times. Nothing like that, nothing so . . . crude."

"Okay," she said. Then she raised her head suddenly so that her lips were inches from his and her eyes staring directly into his eyes in what she was convinced was the ultimate in seductiveness.

"You keep talking about her breasts," she said. "What's so great about her breasts?"

"They're magnificent."

"Don't you like my breasts?"

"Of course I do. Yours are small and perfect, hers are large and perfect. Both are excellent in two different manners."

She pouted. "I don't think you like my breasts any more, Dean."

"Don't be silly. Haven't I demonstrated my fondness for them adequately in the past?"

Her mouth moved closer to his and her voice was huskier than ever. "Prove how much you like them," she coaxed. "Prove it to me, Dean."

He smiled. Obligingly he unbuttoned her blouse, then unclasped her bra. Her breasts were small but perfectly shaped and firm, with small pink nipples that stiffened as he stroked them.

Without warning he lowered his mouth to one breast and took the nipple between his teeth. He bit it, hard, and the mixture of pain and pleasure that went through her was excruciating. She knotted her fingers in his hair and held his head taut against her small young breast.

"Take me," she said. "Right here in the living room on the floor. Right here, Dean. I've got to have you right here and right now and I can't stand to wait."

"I'll be too weak for Miss Hobson."

"Not you," she said. "Not you, Dean. You've got enough for twenty women. You've got plenty, Dean. Give me some of it. Give me some right this minute before I go completely out of my mind."

He pushed her away and made her stand up. This cooled her off momentarily but a second later his hands were on her breasts again and she was being driven wild.

"Take off your clothes," he ordered.

She whipped off her clothing as fast as she could, letting everything fall to the floor. He undressed at a slightly more leisurely pace and she stood naked in the middle of the floor, waiting impatiently for him. When he was nude she threw herself down on the rug and got into position for him, her hips already churning spasmodically and the sweat breaking out on her forehead and in the valley between her breasts.

"Hurry," she moaned. "Come on!"

He laughed. "My God," he said. "Not on the floor. Not in mid-afternoon on the living room floor."

"Dean!"

"Not on the floor," he repeated. "It's different in the cellar. The floor is padded there. It's made for this sort of thing, whereas here—"

"Dean, damn you!"

"Get up."

She sat upon the floor and wrapped her hands around her legs. "You can't do this to me," she whimpered. "You can't get me all hot like this and expect me to cool off when you snap your fingers."

"Who said anything about your cooling off?"

"But—"

"I just told you to get up."

Puzzled, she stood up. He held out his arms for her and she ran to him, pressing her nude body against his and rubbing up against him desperately. She was getting him excited now as well and she was glad, glad that he couldn't remain cold to her. She did something with one hand and he pressed her to him in passion.

"Dean—"

"Now," he said, disengaging himself. "Now maybe you'll see what I meant when I told you to get up. We've never done it in a chair, have we?"

He sat down in the easy chair and drew her into his lap. She didn't know exactly what to do at first but he showed her how to sit and how to arrange herself.

"Now," he said. "How do you like it?"

"Dean—"

Her hips rolled in the movements of love and her passion welled up and spilled over. She couldn't think, couldn't breathe, couldn't do anything but move with him and with her passion and respond to the forces that were working within the confines of her hot body.

"Bitch. How do you like it, you rotten perverted little bitch?"

"Oh, Dean—"

"Bitch!"

He slapped her. It hurt, and then he did something else to her that hurt even more, something that was so painful that she couldn't help crying out in pain and shock and alarm and, simultaneously, excitement. He did it again and it hurt but it was good, so good, and she spoke his name again and again.

"Tell me about it. Tell me how it feels, you despicable little slut."

"It feels good."

"Tell me about it."

"Dean," she moaned. "God, Dean. Oh, Dean, it's so good, so wonderful, so perfect—"

It went on, went on longer than could possibly be possible, went on for what seemed to be forever with the pain and pleasure increasing side by side and hand in hand until she couldn't take it any longer.

And then everything exploded and she lay limp and moist and

exhausted, a bundle of sweaty sated lust and moist spent passion in his arms.

Her body hurt but the hurt was overshadowed by the gentle feeling of happiness that came from being wanted and from being taken with skill and strength and passion. Next to this the pain was inconsequential; the satisfaction was the only thing that mattered.

CHAPTER 5

While Bonnie Leigh was copulating in the easy chair in Dean Hanson's living room on State Street, Mary Hobson was looking for her. She had expected to find Bonnie at school that day, and looked for her in all the places where Bonnie was most likely to be found without finding any trace of her. Then she learned from one person that Bonnie had reported to her teacher that she was sick, and learned from another person that Bonnie was not really sick at all.

She was in her sixth hour study hall now and it gave her a chance to think. She had been looking for Bonnie in order to tell her that she had changed her mind, that she just couldn't go to the club meeting that night. Her sleep the night before had been nervous and jerky—she lay for hours tossing and turning, and it seemed as though a minute after she finally dropped off to sleep the clock on the table at the side of her bed was ringing its silly head off to tell her that it was time to get out of bed and get dressed and go to school.

When she woke up her mind was set—she couldn't go to the meeting of the Unicorns. It wasn't right no matter what kind of meeting it was, she couldn't just up and go without telling Ed. If she had to keep it a secret from him there was something wrong with it, and if there was something wrong with it she could live without it, and if it was something she could live without there was no point in going through with it.

But during the time that she looked unsuccessfully for Bonnie her clear-cut decision became a good bit blurred around the edges. But what really sent her reeling was when Ed told her over lunch about his conversation with his history teacher, Mr. Schwerner.

Although they had never said so in so many words, Mary had taken it for granted that she and Ed would both go to Boston University. Now Ed told her out of the clear blue sky that, not only was he not going to Boston University, but he was very possibly going someplace miles away from her, some jerkwater college out in the middle of nowhere. And she didn't know how to react.

Was this all she meant to him? Oh, he said, they would see each other over vacations, and during the summer, and wherever she was she could come up to wherever he was for a weekend now and then. That was damned nice of him, she thought. Real sweet. It didn't even occur to him that she could go wherever he went, any more that it occurred to him that she wanted to be with him every day and not on vacations and weekends.

But maybe that was because he didn't want her. He wanted her to be around when he felt like seeing her and that was all, wanted her as a steady date without having any responsibility on his part. When he talked about how she could date other boys while they were apart she felt like hitting the ceiling. And now she realized why he had said that. It was because he was looking forward to dating other girls, more exciting girls, and he couldn't do this while he had her hanging around his neck.

So now she wasn't sure about passing up the club meeting. It wasn't as if anything was going to happen to her. She would just be there and get an idea what it was like and see the movie. The idea of the movie interested her and she wondered what it would be like. Maybe it would just be one of those burlesque things they advertised in the magazines her father brought home occasionally where the girl took off her clothes and danced around a little. But she had a hunch it was something more than that—something with people "doing things" to each other.

She hoped that was what it would be. She wanted to see what they would do, how they would do it. Her curiosity shamed her a little but she rationalized it as a perfectly normal curiosity and then it didn't bother her any more. It was, she decided, no different from reading the sexy books she and her friends had devoured when they were just beginning to learn what sex was all about.

Maybe Bonnie was right and Ed was a stuffed shirt. The thought popped into her head out of the blue and she was ashamed of it, feeling somehow disloyal. But maybe he was—so hot on being a hotshot lawyer and so prudish about anything and everything.

By the time the bell rang and signaled the end of the sixth hour study hall she had made up her mind. She would go to the meeting of the Unicorns.

"You know about the meeting?" Ruthellen Perkins asked Jack Lacey. She was a slender girl with dark red hair that framed a thin, almost ascetic face. Her eyes were sunken and her arms and legs were very thin. Hanson, the first time he made love to her, kept whispering "Vampire, vampire" into her ear.

"I know about it."

"You know about our special guest?"

"You mean Mary?" Lacey, who was fat and freckled and foolish and who looked younger than he was and infinitely more innocent than he was, rubbed his fat hands together and grinned an obscene grin.

"I know about her," he said. "And I'll tell you, I'm dying to get into that little one. You ever get a load of the boobs on her?"

"How could I help it?" asked Ruthellen, who was flat as a flounder and not exactly pleased by the fact. "Her tits walk into a room five minutes before the rest of her."

"Don't put her down for that. It's nice that way. Can't have too much of a good thing."

"Well, don't get too excited about it, fellow."

"Why not?"

"Because you may not be getting anything from her."

"Don't be silly—everybody loves a fat man. Didn't you know that?"

"I mean it," Ruthellen said. "She's just coming along for the ride."

"So am I."

Ruthellen shook her head impatiently. "Clod," she said. "I'm trying to tell you what Bonnie told me. Mary's just coming to look the club over and see what it's like. She's not joining or anything."

"You're kidding."

"Ask anybody."

"You're nuts," Lacey insisted. "After Dean works on her for a few minutes she'll be climbing the walls and begging every guy in the room to feed it to her. A gal like her was born with an itch."

"An itch? Where?"

He showed her and she giggled.

"Well," he said, "if she's not available, I could do worse than settle for you. In fact, I kind of have an itch for you myself. A nice private little itch."

"Here?"

"You said it."

"Why me?" she teased. "I can't compete with your Mary Hobson in the boob department."

"Boobs," he said solemnly, "aren't everything."

"I'm glad to hear that. I kind of go for you myself."

"Really?"

"Really."

"How come? I'm just a fat slob. There are plenty of better-looking guys around."

"Nope," she assured him. "You're the best looking one in the club."

"You're nuts."

"I mean it."

"You must be nuts. What's good looking about me?"

"Jack," she said, touching him, "don't you know what they say in the ads? It's what's up front that counts."

"Mary? What time should I drop by tonight?"

It was Ed and she almost told him to come over whenever he wanted until it dawned on her that she was going to the meeting.

"Not tonight," she said. "I'm going out with a couple of girls tonight. Are we going to the show tomorrow night?"

"Guess so. We always do on Friday. What's up for you tonight?"

"Nothing much. Just going to see some of the girls."

He didn't push it—if he had she might have skipped the whole thing. He said something unimportant and she said something unimportant and they made small talk for a few minutes and then he hung up.

After she and her mother had finished doing the dishes she went upstairs to change. She wasn't too sure just what you wore to a sex club meeting but she didn't think it was a problem her mother could help her out with, so she selected a pale green sweater and a black skirt, figuring she couldn't be too out of place dressed like that. She dressed in a hurry, left the house in a hurry, and was outside by 7:30.

It was too early. She went back into the house, picked up a movie magazine and spent twenty minutes turning the pages without reading anything in particular. Then it was time to go and she left the house and walked toward State Street.

On the way she thought about the conversation with Ed. She had asked him if they were going to the show and he said that he guessed so, that they always did on Friday night. There was only one movie theater in Palmer and still they went to it religiously, whether they were showing a western, which she invariably hated, or a musical, which he invariably hated, or a war picture, which both of them invariably hated. Friday night was movie night and that was all there was to do. Whether they felt like going to the show didn't enter into it. That was what they had done for over a year and it was probably what they would do until they graduated.

Dull, she thought. The same damned dull thing every week and there was no way to change it. Maybe the Unicorns had the right idea. Maybe . . .

She walked on, turning a corner, crossing a street, getting closer to the house on State Street. Something was gnawing at her mind but she couldn't identify it; resolutely she forced it from her mind and pursued other trains of thought.

It was going to be a dark night, she saw. All day the sky had been overcast and now there would be neither moon nor stars. She liked the night better than the day and she liked the night when it was dark. It was better that way.

When she came to Hanson's house she walked to the front door and hesitated on the door step. All the lights were out and she thought wildly for an instant that Bonnie had sent her on a wild goose chase.

Then she rang the bell. She waited for three seconds that seemed like thirty minutes and the door opened.

Chapter 6

Dean Hanson's basement was the last word in luxury. The plush feeling existed despite the utter absence of anything that might be classified as furniture. The big room where Bonnie had led her was totally lacking in chairs, tables, sofas, or anything of the sort.

The walls and ceiling were painted a rich deep blue that looked vaguely purple under the dim red lights. The carpeting that covered the floor was wine-red and seemed to be a foot thick—actually the carpet, while luxurious and costly enough, was only the thickness of any good carpet. The fact that a four-inch layer of mattress separated the rug from the floor was responsible for the illusion.

The mattress material made chairs and sofas unnecessary. Everyone was sitting on the floor when she arrived and every head turned toward her and Bonnie. A tall thin man whom she dimly recognized as Dean Hanson rushed over to greet her while the rest of them remained seated on the floor.

"Mary!" He took her hand graciously and smiled warmly at her. "I'm so glad you could come. I think you know everybody here, don't you?"

She did. Betty Jo Meltzer and Moose Gardens sat in one corner, the diminutive brunette looking ridiculous next to the huge bulk of Moose. Jack Lacey, who had a bad case of acne, sat with his arms around Gladys Kent, who was missing one of her teeth in front and who, consequently, had talked with a lisp for as long as anyone could remember. The boys had always seemed to think that the lisp was cute; Mary had always thought it was childish and stupid.

Lesley Banks, a noisy blonde who viewed the world through rose-colored glasses, sat on the lap of Dave Carson, a quiet and studious boy who viewed the world myopically through thick-lensed glasses that kept slipping down on his nose. Ruthellen and Larry Prince were necking noisily by the far wall and Larry's slender fingers were busy stroking her pudgy young breasts. This bothered Mary a little but on second thought it was nothing worse than what usually went on in the back of a car after a dance. Anne Kessler and Al Marshall were paired off, as were Ray Saltonstall and Judy Simmons. Bonnie seemed to be left alone, or perhaps she was waiting for Hanson to join her. Mary couldn't tell.

"The projector's all set up," Hanson was telling her. "We'll get underway in a moment or so. Fortunately it's a model that doesn't require any manual operation—all I do is throw a switch and it runs by itself. The screen's on the wall right over there."

She looked at the screen. In a moment or two she would watch a movie unlike anything she had ever seen before. She wondered what it would be like.

Hanson handed her a twelve-ounce tumbler filled with a liquid that looked like grape juice. "Here," he said, "have a drink."

"I don't drink."

He laughed. "We never have anything alcoholic here," he

assured her. "You needn't worry. This is just grape juice. Sometimes it's rather nice to have something to sip during the movie."

She hesitated, wondering if he was telling her the truth. But there seemed little point for him to lie to her—if it wasn't grape juice she would find out just by tasting it. She looked around the room again and noticed that everybody else had a glass of the stuff. Most of the glasses had already been emptied but some were partially filled with the liquid.

"Taste it," he urged. She did and it was grape juice, very good grape juice. She found out that she was thirsty and drained half the tumbler in a swallow.

Grape juice has a very strong taste to it. At college parties it is frequently mixed with vodka because it conceals the taste of the vodka better than any other juice can. In this case the grape juice concealed the taste of something else—an aphrodisiac that performed two functions admirably, both heightening sexual response and dispersing sexual inhibition with considerable facility. The aphrodisiac known as Mexican Love Powder, has a strong taste of its own which is rather unpleasant to most people.

But all Mary tasted was the grape juice.

"Sit right here," Hanson suggested, showing her to a spot directly in front of the screen. "I'll be back in a second or two."

She sat down. Seconds later Hanson flicked a switch and the room was plunged into pitch-black darkness. Then another switch was flicked and the movie began. Mary took a deep breath and made herself comfortable on the floor. As Hanson sat down next to her and as the title, *The Edge of Passion*, was flashed upon the screen, she raised the tumbler to her lips and drank the rest of the grape juice.

The woman is sitting on the edge of a double bed. She is a tall blonde with long hair and she is wearing a thin negligee. She faces the camera and her lips are smiling gently. She is a very lovely woman.

Very slowly she opens the negligee. She yawns and stretches, revealing her body to the camera. Her very large breasts are smooth and pink and perfectly formed. Her legs are long and shapely. Her thighs are full and she draws them apart, then presses them tight together, then parts them once again.

The camera dollies in for a close-up of the woman's breasts. Obligingly she cups them in her hands and raises each in turn to her mouth. The camera moves in still closer to show full red lips surrounding a pink nipple and caressing it diligently.

The camera pans over an expanse of golden flesh, It focuses on the woman's thighs while she caresses them.

Ruthellen Perkins couldn't stand it any more. "I can't wait," she whispered, very fiercely and very softly all at once.

Jack Lacey nodded. He was perspiring freely and he didn't trust himself to speak.

"Usually I can wait," she said. "But not this time. I'm going crazy."

He nodded again.

"But I don't want to miss any of it," she went on. "I want to do it but I don't want to take my eyes off the screen."

His hands ran the length of her body. His eyes were on the screen but his hands were on her and they were driving her wild.

"What can we do?"

"Take your clothes off," he ordered.

"But—"

"We'll find a way."

They undressed quickly in the darkness, still keeping their eyes on the screen and on the fascinating drama that was unfolding there in full unblushing color. When they were naked he began to stroke her again. Her hands wandered over his body and it was obvious that they could never manage to wait until the film ended.

He showed her how to kneel facing the screen. He touched her some more and she quivered.

"I think," he whispered softly, suiting his actions to his words, "I think the best way to approach this problem is from the rear."

The woman goes through her whole repertoire. Her performance runs the gamut of autoerotic practice and a whole arsenal of imaginative devices are employed in the happy process of self-titillation.

This is not enough.

The camera turns for a shot of the door to the room to indicate that someone is knocking on it. The woman smiles and walks to the door, wrapping her negligee around her as she walks. She opens the door and there is a man standing there.

SUBTITLE: "COME INSIDE."

The man enters. He looks approvingly on the woman, his eyes going from her face to her feet. He smiles, then she smiles.

SUBTITLE: "I'M SELLING BRUSHES."

Woman seems to express interest. Man takes brush from sample case. The brush is long and thin. The man gives it to the women who handles it admiringly.

The woman sits on the edge of the bed. She opens her negligee all the way. The camera dollies in for a close-up as the woman puts the brush to a use for which it was probably never intended by its manufacturer.

Close-up of the woman's face.

Close-up of the man's face.

Close-up of the woman using the brush.

SUBTITLE: "HAVEN'T YOU GOT ANYTHING THAT WILL DO THE JOB BETTER?"

Chapter 7

Mary had not moved since the picture began. She sat very still, her legs curled in front of her, her hands in her lap, her back straight and her eyes on the screen. From time to time her brain issued urgent commands to her eyes to turn from the screen, just as they commanded her legs to uncurl and carry her out of there. But some vital link in the chain of command from brain to organs was severed perhaps by the aphrodisiacal grape juice and perhaps by her own suddenly irresistible sexual desires.

Her brain was whirling, her body burning with new thoughts and new impulses and hungers which had never been this urgent before. As the movie progressed from simple nudity to complex obscenity her feelings deepened and intensified beyond anything she had ever imagined. She watched the woman, first alone and then with the man, and no power on earth could have prevented her first from watching transfixed and then, ultimately, from responding.

She felt a hand upon her breast.

Then another hand on the other breast.

At first the hands merely held her. Where they touched her she felt warm, very warm, as if her breasts were burning up from inside. The hands that held her seemed to come from nowhere although she realized dimly in a hidden part of her brain that they were attached to arms which reached around her from behind. But in her mind she saw not the arms but only the hands, the strong and certain hands that were setting her breasts on fire.

The hands began to move.

Slowly at first and then more dexterously the hands began to manipulate her firm and perfect breasts. The hands kneaded the warm flesh expertly and the sensations that coursed through her body were fantastic ones. She had never felt like this, never before. Ed hadn't made her feel like this. No one ever could have made her feel like this. She wanted to squirm, to writhe, to let her whole body respond completely to the new forces that were gushing through her veins and arteries and capillaries and making her feel as she had never felt before.

But she could not move. She could do nothing but sit as she was sitting and watch as she was watching while the man on the screen did incredible things to the beautiful blonde woman. As he did these things it seemed to Mary as though he was doing them not to the woman but to her herself and she grew increasingly more excited with every iota of activity that took place on the screen.

The hidden part of her mind began to fight. Somebody's feeling you up, that part of her mind said. Somebody's feeling you up, somebody has his hot little hands on your sweater and pretty soon something's going to happen. You better watch out.

She didn't listen.

And very shortly thereafter the hands did try something else. They released her breasts and began to tug at the bottom of her sweater. Even the feeling of the material being pulled free of her skirt was exciting, and when finally the sweater had been pulled over her head—obscuring for just a few seconds her view of the screen—she felt freer, more alive.

And when hands were on her breasts, touching her through the thin protection of the flimsy white bra, it was better. Much better. No sweater to get in the way, less material between those devilish hands and those burning breasts. She could feel the individual fingers now as they fondled and stroked her.

The hands left her breasts.

Fooled around with the clasp of the bra.

Mastered the clasp.

Slipped the bra from her, the straps from her shoulders, freed her breasts.

And returned to them, cupped them, the bare hands full now with her bare flesh and touching, stroking, squeezing, fondling.

And God in Heaven how good it felt!

The right nipple was between the thumb and forefinger of the right hand. The left nipple was between the thumb and forefinger of the left hand. And the hands were touching and pinching and the nipples were wondrously and gloriously alive and afire.

Another pair of hands took hold of her right leg and drew it straight out in front of her. Still another pair of hands did the same thing to her left leg. The two pairs of hands removed her shoes, pulled off her socks, stroked her small feet and trim ankles and neatly rounded calves. The two pairs of hands reached under her skirt and moved farther and farther up along her thighs.

There were three people touching her, three boys busy exciting her. It was, she thought dreamily, very pleasant to be caressed by three boys at once.

On the screen the man did something unspeakable to the woman. She seemed to be enjoying it tremendously.

And the hands went on with their work.

Her skirt was unbuttoned. Fingers worked at the zipper and got it open. Then the six hands together managed the task of lifting her a few inches from the floor so that first her skirt and then her panties could be drawn ever so gently from her.

Now she was naked.

As naked as the blonde woman on the screen.

And the hands, the devilish hands, resumed with skill their devilish and clever and cunning and stimulating tasks of exciting her more and more and more, stroking breasts and hip and thigh, rubbing her soft flat tummy, handling her every place and exploring every hidden and secret part of her body.

A mouth joined the hands. A mouth was kissing one breast, a moist tongue caressing a nipple, and she could not tell whether the mouth belonged to the owner of one of the pairs of hands or whether a fourth caresser had entered into the fray.

It seemed unimportant.

She went on sitting very still while her passion mounted to heights she had never dreamed of. She went on being caressed and excited while hands and lips burned her up and while that distant part of her mind screamed in stony silence, wondering what in the name of Heaven or Hell was going to happen to her.

The man and woman have made love three times. They are now lying in each other's arms on top of the bed. The man is stroking the woman's body familiarly with one hand; she is doing intimate things to him at the same time. Similar vacuous grins cover both their faces.

Close-up of the man's hand on the woman's breast. The camera pans to follow the hand as it strokes the woman, then moves up for a shot of her face which is contorted in an expression of what is supposed to be sublime passion.

Medium shot of the door.

Shot of the man and woman in state of shock.

SUBTITLE: "WHO'S THAT AT THE DOOR?"

Man, nude, rushes into the closet. Woman hurriedly dons her negligee and answers the door. The door opens to reveal a short, slender girl who is approximately fourteen years old. The girl is wearing a Girl Scouts uniform and carries a carton in one hand. Her hair is dark brown and she is wearing no makeup.

SUBTITLE: "WOULD YOU LIKE TO BUY SOME GIRL SCOUT COOKIES?"

Shot of woman laughing.

SUBTITLE: "GO AWAY."

Girl begins crying. Her jacket is torn and her shoes scuffed to suggest poverty.

SUBTITLE: "I HAVE TO SELL MY COOKIES."

Close-up of woman's face. Her expression suggests that she has just been visited with a marvelous idea.

SUBTITLE: "IF YOU DO EXACTLY WHAT WE TELL YOU TO DO WE WILL BUY YOUR COOKIES."

The girl nods, smiling. The woman motions her inside, then closes the door. She takes off the girl's jacket and has her sit down on the edge of the bed. Then the woman turns to the door of the closet.

SUBTITLE: "YOU CAN COME OUT NOW. IT'S ALL RIGHT."

Medium shot of man, nude, coming from closet. Close-up of girl's face as she looks at him, then turns away in obvious embarrassment.

SUBTITLE: "YOU WANT US TO BUY YOUR COOKIES, DON'T YOU?"

Man and woman sit on bed on either side of girl. They begin to undress her. The girl acts humiliated but offers them no resistance as they remove her clothing.

Moose Gardens whispered: "Oh honey you're wonderful. You're the absolute end of the world. Oh God in Heaven what you do to me."

Betty Jo Meltzer said nothing.

Moose Gardens whispered: "Don't stop, baby. Sweet little baby. My sweet baby. It's so good. God in Heaven it's good."

Betty Jo Meltzer said nothing.

Moose Gardens whispered: "Keep it up, sweet. Keep it up, you sweet little tiny bundle of sex. Keep it up because if you stop now I'll rip your goddamned little head off, you sweet thing you."

Betty Jo Meltzer said nothing.

Moose Gardens whispered: "Ohhh. Ohhh God. Nothing ever felt like this. You're sweet, baby. You're so sweet. Nobody else was ever this sweet."

Betty Jo Meltzer said nothing.

Which was quite natural.

With what she was doing, conversation would have been quite impossible.

• • •

Mary couldn't see the screen any more.

She could not see the screen because she was lying flat on her back. Even if she had been seated as before, however, it would have been impossible for her to see the screen. Her eyes were closed.

Besides, she didn't want to see. Seeing and tasting and hearing and smelling were all right in their place, but at the moment only one form of sensation seemed important to her.

Touch.

She was lying on her back now with her feet straight out in front of her and her arms at her sides. The floor beneath her felt as comfortable and as soft as her own bed. The hands that touched and prodded, the mouths that kissed, felt absolutely one hundred per cent out of this world.

Up to this point she had been silent. Up to this point she had been motionless. But now, with touch taking over completely and all the other senses being shut out, she could no longer remain silent or motionless.

Weird animalistic moans that originated deep within her throat ripped into the air. Her body began to squirm and writhe like a Haitian dancer and her hips churned in spasms of sheer sex.

The caresses continued. The longer they went on and the bolder they became, the less sufficient they were to meet the demands of her newly aroused body. Something radical was needed, something different.

She did not have long to wait.

One of the pairs of hands rearranged each leg in turn so that they were bent at the knee, the thighs parted. Another pair of hands elevated her and placed a pillow beneath her.

The altar had been prepared.

Now the sacrifice would be made.

Although she did not know one lover from the next, it was Hanson who took her first. A jet of agony screamed through her body, pierced her and tore her apart like a cannon in a deserted churchyard, burned like a fiery sword through her heart and mind and body. She screamed with her pain and the scream bounced from wall to wall and echoed in the basement room.

It was happening.

She felt the man moving upon and within her, felt herself miraculously responding, miraculously enjoying what was happening to her, miraculously moving and writhing and turning and twisting, miraculously turning pain to pleasure and savoring every sensation, every vibration, every feeling and every bit of the experience.

Instinctively her body did what it was supposed to do. Instinctively she rolled and instinctively her arms wound around Hanson's middle. She hugged him and moved with him and pulled him hard against her.

Hanson finished before she did. While she was still straining for a climax he left her, left her to twist and writhe alone.

But not for long.

Because a second after he had left her another boy had joined her, taking Hanson's place in the overall scheme of things. He moved and she moved and then, finally, the whole damned world moved and it happened.

It was even better than she had dreamed it would be.

But she did not have long to think about it, to think how good it was, because as soon as it happened the second boy was leaving her and a third boy was replacing him. And it began to begin again, began to happen again, and now her whole brain turned itself off and only her body remained in the reeling world.

First the woman lies down on the bed. She makes the girl recline on top of her so that the girl's back is upon the woman's stomach. She holds the girl in this position while the man makes love to the girl.

SUBTITLE: "NOW IT'S MY TURN."

The roles are reversed. The man lies down as the woman has done. The girl lies on top of the man and the woman makes love to the girl. During both of these episodes the camera moves from one spot to the other, now dollying in for close-ups of various areas of various bodies, now moving back for medium shots of the overall tableaux. All three participants maintain graphic facial expressions throughout; the man and woman of supreme pleasure, the girl of pain and humiliation. Despite the ostensible pain and humiliation, at no point does the girl offer the slightest degree of even token resistance.

The fun and games proceed at a pace that is a great credit to the imagination of the anonymous scenarist and a tribute to the endurance of the actors themselves. They race through a variety at perverted acts. Both the man and the woman have their fun with the girl. Occasionally they make love to her simultaneously. Intermittently they coerce her to perform various acts upon them.

FINALE:

The girl, understandably exhausted, stretches out on the bed. She closes her eyes and seems to relax. The camera dollies back for a long

shot as the man and woman clamber to a more-or-less standing po-
sition upon the bed.

The woman stands at the girl's head, the man at her feet. They
reach across the girl's body and shake hands rather incongruously.
SUBTITLE: THE END

Eight men made love to Mary Hobson. Not men, really. Boys. Seven boys and a man, if you call Dean Hanson a man. Eight boys, if you prefer to think in terms of his emotional rather than chronological development.

It was not a rape. At no point in the proceedings did Mary Hobson offer any resistance whatsoever. After the movie had ended and the lights had been turned on and all the Unicorns had gathered around to watch her initiation, even then she continued to want it to be done to her and to participate most actively in the affair.

One after the other they took her. One after the other they took their pleasure with her, and when all of them had finished she passed out. She lay very still on the floor, an inert bundle of abused female flesh.

Carefully and considerately they took her to the bathroom and washed her and dried her. Carefully and considerately they dressed her in her own clothes once again, lipsticked her mouth and rouged her cheeks. Carefully and considerately they bundled her into Dean Hanson's Lincoln and drove her to her own home.

They took her key from her purse and unlocked her door. Her family was sound asleep and they had no difficulty carrying her upstairs and taking her to her room. There they undressed her again, considered but decided against violating her once more on her own little bed, hung up her clothing and tucked her into bed.

They left and she slept.

She woke up in the morning. She awoke very early because when the drug wore off it wore off with a bang and left her wide awake. She opened her eyes, and for a moment everything was all right.

Then she remembered and the world went to hell.

She remembered it all in one quick flash of horror. She remembered everything from beginning to end and her stomach churned. She raced to the bathroom and threw up over and over again.

How had it happened? How had anything like that happened to her?

How had she permitted it to happen?

She went back to her bed, lay on it this time with her face down, and began to cry into the feathery softness of her pillow.

CHAPTER 8

New England Indian Summer is more than the title of a very excellent literary history by Van Wyck Brooks. It is also an accepted fact. Every so often in New England when the summer comes to an official close it is only just getting started.

There's a cooling-off period after August gives up the ghost. For a few days the weather is quite brisk and the sky overcast. Then the sun comes up out of the east in a flash of glory and the clouds melt into the blueness of the sky and the leaves on the trees sway in gentle breezes. This is New England Indian Summer and it is quite definitely a joy to behold.

It began that morning. The sky was clear at dawn and the sun was hot. By seven-fifteen the air was warm and the students who trooped merrily or plodded wearily to Nathan Palmer High School left their jackets at home because they didn't need them now. The wise birds who weren't misled by preliminary signs of winter were busy chasing the dumb worms around the green lawns. The morning was pleasantly bright, the dawn nicely dewpearled, God was obviously in his heaven and all was right with the world.

The hell it was.

•   •   •

If a shock is great enough, the body endures it in one of two manners. Either the body experiencing the shock goes into some form of withdrawal such as schizophrenia or hysteria or the body seems to bury the shock completely, acting in a normal fashion and living through a certain period of time in a normal manner.

Mary Hobson reacted in the second fashion. After she had been violently sick to her stomach a number of times she took a prolonged bath and scrubbed herself until her skin burned. Then she dressed as usual, went downstairs as usual, chatted politely and noncommittally with her parents as usual, made her way through a glass of pineapple-grapefruit juice, a bowl of corn flakes, and a glass of milk as usual, and walked as usual out of her house and off down the street toward the school.

On the outside nothing seemed to be different in her look, her conversation, her walk. On the inside everything was very different. Everything was upside down, as a matter of fact, and while she walked with a sure step and spoke with a deft tongue, she felt as though at any moment she would fall flat on her face and bawl like a baby.

It was still not quite possible for her to realize just what she had done and just what had been done to her in the basement of Dean Hanson's home on State Street. She knew the bare facts of the evening's entertainment—that she had watched a vile movie and had submitted more than willfully to the embraces of eight males, that she had enjoyed these embraces as much as her eight embracers had enjoyed them, that at last she had passed out and had been taken home to wake up mercifully alone in her own bed. This much she knew, but her knowledge of it was limited. She knew it in much the same fashion that a soldier with a bullet in his chest knows that he is about to die. He may accept the fact that death is minutes or seconds away from him, that no reprieve is possible, that at any moment he will cease to exist. But the face of Death is hidden from him. He has no understanding of what Death is, of what it will feel like to be dead, of just how tremendous a thing has happened to him. Perhaps the merciful thing about such a quick and sudden death is the lack of time given to him to contemplate his situation.

Mary Hobson knew that she had participated in what could only be called a perverted orgy. She knew that she was no longer a virgin, no longer a good girl, no longer a person worthy of the respect either of others or, more important, of herself. These things she knew but she knew them by rote. A more perceptive understanding of just what had become of her came later.

Part of this comprehension came when Al Marshall gave her a knowing smile in the hallway. More came when another boy, not one of the Unicorns but a near-stranger named Marty Jukovsky, brushed by her on her way to algebra. She shrank from his touch although he had not touched her intentionally at all and the mere fact of contact with a male, however so slight and however so innocent, made her feel dirty inside.

Slowly understanding sank in. Betty Jo Meltzer winked at her and she felt the blood rush to her face. A boy in the hallway told a mildly obscene joke about a bald-headed mouse to another boy in the hallway. She overheard the tail end of it and felt like fainting.

But the full force of it hit her when, standing in front of the doorway to the lunchroom, she saw Ed Bainbridge and Bonnie Leigh approaching, one from the left and the other from the right. She turned one way, then the other. Her mouth dropped open and the book that she had been holding in her left hand fell unnoticed to the floor.

She ran.

She did not know where she was going but her feet led her to the girl's washroom. The room was empty and she paced back and forth from one wall to another, not knowing why she was there or what she was going to do, knowing simply that she couldn't go out, couldn't face Ed, couldn't bear to see Bonnie, couldn't go anywhere or do anything.

She felt dirty.

Filthy.

And the dirt that seemed to cover her inside and out was not dirt that could be washed off or thrown up. It was deep, too deep to yield to soap or an emetic. The filthiness was a part of her.

Because she had submitted willingly, far too willingly. It wasn't as if she had been the victim of a rape, wasn't as if boys had pinned her thighs apart and held her arms down while they took her. Her legs had been free, free to wind around a boy and hold him close to her. Her arms had been free as well—free to touch a boy, to caress him, to hold him close while he took her.

How could she face Ed? No wonder she had found him dull, spiritless, cold. No wonder she had agreed in silence when Bonnie had accused him of being a stuffed shirt. To girls like herself and Bonnie, any man was a stuffed shirt if he didn't want to roll around on a cellar floor with a group of perverts.

Ed wasn't stuffy. He wasn't cold, either. He was only so in comparison with her, and she was perverted and oversexed and all the other words that had been no more than words until she saw how they applied in her own case. Now they were labels, unpleasant labels, horrifying labels as she applied them to herself and winced under the lash of them.

Ed was too good for her. One night had changed her from a good girl into a bad girl, changed her from a girl who went steady with Ed Bainbridge and expected to marry Ed Bainbridge to a girl who wasn't fit to talk with him, much less be his steady or his wife.

She shook her head. That, she decided, was not quite correct. Last night hadn't made any tremendous difference, not deep down inside where it counted. If anything it showed her the sort of girl she was, showed her something she had been too blind to see in the past. She had been a bad girl all along, or, if *good* and *bad* were unwieldy terms, an oversexed and perverted girl all along. Last night had enabled her to see herself for what she was. Now she wouldn't have to pretend, wouldn't have to tell herself that Ed was cold when, in fact, it was her own superabundance of warmth that made him seem cold in contrast.

No more pretending.

No more fooling herself.

No more sitting on the couch with Ed, kissing and touching without doing what she yearned to do, "controlling themselves" when control was the last thing she wanted. She almost smiled as she remembered a greeting card they had seen at the drug store. There was a picture of a kid on the front plus the caption *Happy Birthday*. Inside it said *Now you can play with the big kids*.

That was her, all right. Now she could play with the big kids. Now she could join the Unicorns and do what they did, letting herself go, letting her mind subordinate itself to her body, letting out all the stops and living for pleasure and pleasure alone.

But she didn't want that. Instead she wanted the comfort of Ed's arms and the security of Ed's love and the smooth and uncomplicated existence of a girl who knows right from wrong and chooses right, a girl who plays the game according to the rules, who goes to church on Sundays, who does her work in school and graduates and marries Ed and raises a family and lives happily ever after.

That was what she wanted.

It was what she was firmly convinced would never be what she wound up with.

And, because what she wanted was not what she seemed to possess, and because all in all she was a very young girl and a very bewildered little girl, she sat down on a toilet seat and closed the door and put her face in her hands and cried.

Chapter 9

Ed started after her when she headed for the washroom. The fact that her refuge was where it was more or less stopped him; he was only a few steps behind her when the door shut and the sign GIRLS kept him from going any farther. He stood in front of the door hesitantly, knowing something was wrong and completely at sea as to what it might be, wanting to talk to Mary and unsure how he could get a chance to talk to her.

Because, quite obviously, something was radically wrong. While he couldn't pinpoint it, something had been wrong for some time now and he wanted to get to the bottom of it. The way she had behaved when he told her about his conversation with Mr. Schwerner, for example. The way she had seemed way out in left field the last time they had been together, first at the Soda Mill and then in her living room.

Something was very wrong. So many things were piling together, one on top of the other, and he was darned if he could figure out whether it all stemmed from his decision to go out of town to school or from the Unicorns or what. He was stymied.

And somebody was holding his arm.

He whirled around. It was Bonnie, and the way he spun around made her draw back in mock-terror as if she was afraid he was going to take a swing at her.

"Take it easy," she said "I didn't do it."

"Didn't do what?"

"Whatever it was," she said. "Whatever has you so shook up."

She waited for him to tell her what had him so shook up and he shrugged half-heartedly in reply. He didn't particularly go for Bonnie—he never had, and this bit about the Unicorns didn't exactly make her all the more exciting to him.

"Well?"

"I don't know," he said. "She took one look at me and then she ran in here as if the world was coming to an end and she wanted to get out of the way before the sky fell in on top of her. I don't know whether it's something I did or what. It's mixing me up."

Bonnie laughed. She threw her arms back and laughed and her small breasts pushed against the front of the white sleeveless blouse she was wearing. He couldn't help noticing her breasts and it made him feel ill at ease. There was something about knowing that a girl was available that made her all the more exciting. Mary, for instance, was a hell of a lot more attractive than Bonnie would ever be, for his money at least. But he could look at Mary without getting bothered this way, while with Bonnie he kept thinking about things that he shouldn't be thinking about.

"What's so funny?"

"You are," she said. "You men are so self-centered it's a riot. Honest to God, just because she gets a rush call to the john you think you're responsible."

"I don't get it."

"Don't you?"

He shook his head.

"Ed," she said patiently, "every once in a while a girl has to run like crazy to the john. She doesn't have time to say hello to her friends or smile politely like a good little girl. Do you have the slightest idea what I'm talking about now?"

"Nope."

"I'll give you a clue," she said. "This sort of thing happens once a month. Now do you get the message or should I put it in sky-writing?"

"Oh." He felt himself blushing and it irritated him. Menstruation was a perfectly natural thing and he knew it, but when a girl like Bonnie Leigh talked so openly about it he couldn't help feeling embarrassed. It was just the effect she had on him.

"The time to worry," she advised him, "is when she *doesn't* have to run to the can. Then you're in trouble. Or *she's* in trouble, to be accurate about it. Or don't you know what I'm talking about now?"

"I know what you're talking about." She was teasing him and he knew he shouldn't let it get under his skin but he couldn't help it. "I know what you're talking about," he repeated, "and I'd prefer it if you'd find another subject for your conversation. You have no right to talk that way about Mary and I'll thank you to keep talk like that to yourself."

She laughed again. The laughter bothered him but the sight of her breasts pushing against the flimsy bra bothered him even more. He cursed himself silently, wondering why he didn't simply turn and put Bonnie Leigh out of his life for the time being.

"Let's forget Mary," she was saying now. "She'll be in there for a good while, if I'm any judge of feminine hygiene. Let's quit standing in front of the can. It doesn't look very nice, you know."

He turned with her and they headed toward the lunchroom.

Dimly he realized that he had been out-maneuvered. He had been trying to get rid of her and now he was walking with her to the cafeteria. Now there was no graceful way to get out of eating with her and talking some more with her, and that was one thing he was not looking forward to at all.

Mechanically he followed her through the cafeteria line. They filled their plates with tasteless rubbish, the daily cuisine of Nathan Palmer High School, and Bonnie led the way to a table along the far wall. The table was empty, as were the several tables near it. He wished fervently that she had chosen a table in the midst of a batch of other kids. He didn't want to be alone with her if he could possibly help it. But what could he do?

They sat down and started to eat. But she wasn't eating. Instead she was staring thoughtfully at him and it made him uncomfortable. He couldn't eat. He put his food down, annoyed, and turned to her.

"What's the matter?"

She pouted. "I just felt like looking at you. You're nice to look at, Ed. Can't a girl have a little innocent fun?"

"Come off it."

"I'm not kidding, Ed. You do things to me. I sort of flip over you."

He lifted his fork and pretended interest in his food. Then she took hold of his arm above the elbow and squeezed gently.

"Nice," she said admiringly. "Brains and brawn. You've got muscles, Ed. Make a muscle for me. Show me how strong you are."

"Cut it out, will you?"

She grinned. "What's the matter, Ed? Does this excite you

or something? Are you afraid you'll get all excited and then you won't be interested in Mary any more? Is that what you're worried about?"

"Bonnie—"

"I like it when you say my name as though you're mad at me. I like the way it sounds. Say it again."

"Damn it, Bonnie—"

She was still holding his arm. It felt strangely warm where she was holding it.

"That's nice," she murmured. "Now say my last name. I don't even mind if you mispronounce it the way some of the boys do."

"Huh?"

"You know," she prompted. "It's pronounced Bonnie *Lee*, but some of the fellows say it Bonnie *Lay*. I wouldn't mind if you said it that way."

He took a deep breath.

"I wouldn't mind, Ed. I wouldn't mind if you did it to me either. I'd like it if you did it to me."

"Cut it out."

She released his arm. Now her hand was on his thigh and she knew just what to do to excite him. She didn't do anything but run her soft hand up and down his thigh.

That was plenty.

He tried valiantly not to respond. He tried to think about other things but all he could think of was the promise hidden behind Bonnie's words and implicit in Bonnie's soft hand. His mind filled with erotic images of her—Bonnie lying nude on a bed, Bonnie with her arms and legs wide to welcome him, Bonnie doing things with and to him.

"Oh," she whispered. "You like this. I can tell that you like this."

"Stop it."

"Your mouth says stop it," she said. "But another part of you says that what I'm doing is nice. You can't keep secrets from me, Ed. I ought to touch that part of you just to see—"

"Goddamn it!"

"Shhhh! Not so loud, Ed. Not so loud, baby. You know you like it. I bet you'd like to lay me. Wouldn't you? Wouldn't you like to lay me?"

He didn't say a word.

"I'm good, Ed. Baby, I'm good. I've been loved by experts, Ed, Ed honey baby. I'll give you a good time, better than you ever had before. Better than anything anybody else could show you."

His brain whirled. It was ridiculous—she was practically laying him in the middle of the cafeteria with people all over the place, talking like a River Street prostitute and, all at the same time, driving him crazy with her hot little hand. He just wanted to be rid of her but she was intoxicating and he didn't know what to do.

"What's the matter, Ed? You aren't a virgin, are you? Is honey baby a virgin? Hasn't honey baby ever gotten into a girl's pants?"

"Bonnie—"

"Gonna let Bonnie take your cherry, honey baby? Ed, we could go over to my house this afternoon. We could go up in my bedroom and nobody would be home and we could do it on my bed. I've got nice smooth sheets on my bed and the springs don't squeak like they do on my parents' bed. We could be there all afternoon, honey baby, and I could show you what to do if you don't know already, and—"

He pulled his shirt out of his pants, letting it hide the rather tangible evidence of the effect she was having on him. Then he left the table, walking quickly away from her, leaving her there without saying another word to her because he was afraid his voice would be strange and unnatural if he should try to speak.

Lunch was over. He left the lunchroom and headed for the relative security of the classroom, where he could force the images of Bonnie Leigh from his brain. His mind was spinning with unfamiliar desires, desires which he despised more in himself than he did in others, desires which had a frightening effect upon him.

But getting rid of those images proved more difficult than he had imagined. All through the class he kept thinking about Bonnie and what she was offering to him with no strings attached. He was a virgin, and the desire for experience was a strong one. Sometimes, though he struggled against the thought, it bothered him that he was unaware of a whole area of human experience.

Suppose he and Mary got married without his having had sexual relations with another girl. According to what he had read, that could be a very traumatic affair. One book had assured him that the two of them wouldn't know what to do with each other.

And suppose Mary was unsatisfied with him because of his lack of experience. Suppose.

Too many supposes.

The idea of taking Bonnie up on her offer was a very tempting one. He thought of doing it with her on her bed and he felt himself getting excited again. It would be fun—there wasn't any question about that part of it—and it would be an experience, and he certainly wouldn't be cheating Bonnie out of anything she hadn't thrown away a good many times already. The girl was a Unicorn through and through, and evidently very much satisfied with her position in life.

But he would be cheating Mary. He wanted her to remain pure for him, and it only seemed equitable that he retain the same purity for her. It was only right, and he felt also that any experience he might have beforehand might cheapen things later on.

Most of the fellows didn't agree with him. Most of them thought that a strict double standard was the only morally defensible and physically defensible position. Girls should remain virgins until they were married; boys should root around as much as they possibly could. This, inevitably, led to an interesting question—if all the girls were virgins, with whom precisely would all the boys root around?

He didn't believe in double standards. What was right for Mary was right for him. Resolutely he decided that Bonnie could take her charms and keep them. He wouldn't have anything to do with her.

His resolve was firm.

But he still went on thinking about her. He couldn't help it.

Chapter 10

Bonnie was pleased with herself.

She was pleased with life, with the way of the world, and, especially, with Bonnie Leigh. She was very pleased with the way the meeting had gone the night before and even more pleased with the pleasant little conversation she and Ed had just concluded.

Ed, fool that he was, evidently didn't think that he and she would wind up in the same bed. That was what he thought, but she knew better. Mary hadn't thought she would wind up getting gleefully laid at the Unicorn meeting, for example, and she could not have been more wrong. Because gleeful was the word for it, and it had done Bonnie's heart good to see Mary lying on the floor squirming and twisting all over the place with a man on top of her.

It was good Ed had fallen for that line about Mary having her period. It was, she thought, pretty fast thinking on her part, because Mary obviously had headed for the john like a scared rabbit because she was too embarrassed to show her face to the two of them.

Poor Mary. Well, in time she would straighten up and fly right. As soon as she got over feeling guilty, she'd realize that the smartest thing she could do was to relax and enjoy life.

Which was Bonnie's attitude.

Take Ed Bainbridge, for instance. And that, by the way, was precisely what she intended to do. She intended to take Ed Bainbridge and she intended to take him for his cherry and have a damn good time while she was at it. It would be a pleasure all across the board.

She closed her eyes, ignored the class that was being conducted around her, and remembered the meeting. She thought about the action that had taken place on the screen, reviewing the whole movie in detail and savoring every last episode of it. The movie had been the best one the Unicorns had ever seen, the best Bonnie had ever seen, and she felt herself getting excited just going over it in her mind.

Next she remembered what she had watched Mary doing. That had been a thrill, too—Mary must have had one hell of a dose of the love powder, the way she had acted. She was a grand performer.

Bonnie saved the choicest memories for last. The choicest memories concerned what she herself had done and what she herself had had done to her. These were very nice memories and she took a long time remembering everything that there was to remember—caresses, kisses, every type of sensation she had experienced that night.

Then she thought some more about Ed.

He represented something quite different from any of the boys in the club. He wasn't a willing partner as all of them had been. He required a careful and deliberate seduction; the role of seducer was a new one for her and one she found herself rather enjoying. He was so reserved, so cool, but beneath that reserve there was a lot of passion and she would tap it if it killed her.

And it would be fun. Plenty of fun, she decided. Plenty of good clean teenage adolescent juvenile high-school-senior fun.

Thrills.

Kicks.

Dreamily she cast her eyes on the teacher at the front of the classroom, thinking that she ought to feel a sense of kinship with the woman. Because soon she would be a teacher too. She would teach Ed all about it, show him things no woman had ever shown him.

Miss Bonnie Leigh.

Instructor in Physical Education.

Very physical education.

She smiled a secret smile and wondered what it would be like to be first with a boy. Of course it wouldn't be the same thing for a girl to be first with a boy as it was for a boy to be first with a girl. A boy didn't have a hymen to lose. There was no pain or anything like that.

But still she would be willing to bet that it would be different. She hadn't had the chance yet—there had only been one boy taken into the Unicorns and another girl had first crack at him in the time that she had been a member.

But Ed . . .

How long would it take her? She hoped it would not take too long, because she didn't want to wait, and at the same time she didn't want the conquest to be too easy or the value of the prize would be correspondingly lower.

He wanted her already. That much of the battle was won. The

fish was already hooked. At this point it was merely a question of seeing how much of a fight he put up before she succeeded in landing him.

Chapter 11

It took Mary the whole day to make up her mind, took her until halfway through her seventh hour class to clear the confusion from her brain and figure out the proper course of action. The confusion was never entirely gone—it never is, not when there's so much of it rattling around inside your head that you can't see straight or think straight or talk straight—but by and large she knew some of the basic situation and had a fair idea what she ought to do to get herself on the right track.

There were, at the beginning, many possibilities. Too many, and they fell all over themselves, and she fell all over herself at first trying to dope each out in turn. For one thing, she could always pretend that nothing had happened. The only people who knew what she had done last night were the other Unicorns and they certainly weren't going to broadcast the news far and wide.

On the surface this seemed to be the easiest course. If she kept it a secret she could bury it inside and even try to forget it herself. Her relationship with Ed, with her parents, with the world would remain unchanged.

But there were some serious weaknesses in this line of reasoning.

Living with a lie is never easy. The larger the lie, the more difficult it becomes to live with. If she didn't tell Ed, for example, she would always feel the edge of the lie like a knife between them. Their relationship could never be quite the same as it was, and she herself would probably come to love him less as a result of what she was keeping from him.

And if it ever came out, if a doctor or anyone ever discovered the deception, then her life would be a complete and total hell.

Well, that killed that one. Another possibility was the one that had seemed most completely sane to her at first: kicking over whatever traces remained, joining the Unicorns and living for pleasure. She knew enough about herself now to realize that the physical part of that life was in tune with her own oversexed body, but the emotional side of the coin was less appealing. It might well be still harder for her to live with herself and impossible for her to retain any respect for herself if she became that kind of a girl.

The third decision, the one she finally chose, was to tell somebody. It was too big a secret to keep to herself, too much to carry on her own shoulders. She had to tell somebody, had to talk everything out with just one other person, and the obvious person to tell was Ed.

Which was what she decided.

The decision both relieved her and depressed her. Any decision brings a certain measure of relief when the person who has made it has been having difficulty making up his mind. But at the same time she was hardly looking forward to telling Ed. It would be hard enough to tell anybody about something like this, let alone a person like Ed with a hearty contempt for the Unicorns and a narrow attitude toward sex in general. She didn't know how he would react and she couldn't even attempt to predict what he would say or what he would do, or, most important of all, just how he would feel inside about the whole thing.

She would tell him, she vowed, brushing her blonde hair back with one hand and looking at the clock, waiting for the bell to ring and the day's work to come to a welcome close. She would tell him, tell him everything once and for all, and from then on it would be up to him. If he wanted her anyway in spite of what he had learned about her, then she would go to him and they would be together, the two of them against the world. Even if things could never be quite the same for them, even if she couldn't come to him as a virgin, they would still have their love and their relationship would remain an honest one.

And if he didn't want her anymore, if he rejected her now that she was soiled . . . well, she didn't want to think about that if she could possibly help it. If nothing else, she could take it for granted that he would keep her secret. He wasn't the kind of guy to disclose a confidence. From there on her life would be whatever she chose to make it, and she still had the twin choices of joining the Unicorns or making like nothing had happened.

But first she had to tell him.

She had been anxious for the bell to ring, yet when it rang she responded slowly and moved almost languidly. She got up from her seat, gathered her books in her arms and headed for her locker on the first floor. There she left the books she wouldn't need that night and picked up the books she would need. The combination lock on her locker failed to respond the first time around and the second time she manipulated it very carefully, taking more time than she had to take.

She was trying to kill time, of course. Sitting in class waiting for the bell to ring had been its own kind of hell, but now that the class was over and all that she had to do was hurry outside to meet Ed by the front steps she didn't want to move at all.

It was aggravating. When she made her decision and told herself how it was the only right and sensible course of action, it seemed a lot easier than it was turning out to be. Now it was very difficult, very difficult indeed for her to act the way her mind told her to act. Confession, while good for the soul, is tough on the heart and stomach and liver. She wanted desperately to crawl into a quiet hole and disappear from the face of the earth for an absolute minimum of four hundred years.

But she kept going. She tucked her books under her arm, took a deep breath and let it out slowly, straightened her spine and walked briskly to the front doors of Nathan Palmer High School. The air was fresh and as soon as she was outdoors she took another deep breath and held it in her lungs as long as she could.

Indian Summer still reigned in Palmer in all its radiant splendor. The sun was still a gold ball upon a field of blue and it was much brighter and much warmer than it had been when she had walked to school that morning. But the sun's heat and the Indian Summer's radiant splendor were equally lost on her while she made out Ed, his back to her about fifty feet away in the spot where they always met, and walked to him.

"I've been looking for you all day," he told her. "Where have you been hiding?"

"Nowhere special."

"Want to run over to the mill for a soda? I'm rich today."

She shook her head soberly. "Not now," she said. "There's something I want to talk to you about."

"We can talk there."

"It's private."

He looked at her questioningly and she shivered deep inside. This was turning out to be hard right from the start, harder even than she had expected it would be. She took his arm, gripping it a little bit tighter than she had intended to, and began to lead him away from the steps.

"Where are we going?"

"Nowhere."

"But—"

"Ed," she said, "I have something to tell you and I don't know where to begin. I want for us to go for a walk."

He grinned. The grin, in the context of what she knew and what he of course did not know, struck her as somewhat inane.

"Okay with me," he said. "Just lead the way and fill me in as we go along."

She nodded and they walked and for the first five minutes she did not say a word while his expression changed from mild amusement to mild concern and finally to general anxiety.

Then she began to speak.

Chapter 12

Dean Hanson fitted a cigarette into the ivory-and-ebony holder, flipped the switch between the breasts of the girl-shaped cigarette lighter and lit the cigarette. He inhaled deeply, exhaled thoroughly, and sat motionless in his chair while the smoke rose slowly to the high ceiling of his living room.

Dean Hanson's nerves were on edge. This was more than a little irritating, since one of his main objectives in life was to avoid any situation which could set his nerves on edge. And yet he had to admit that the edginess itself was exhilarating, in a way. His nervousness was almost a welcome change from the overwhelming blanket of security which had been having a suffocating effect upon him lately.

And it was all attributable to Mary Hobson.

Memories of Mary Hobson warmed him. Recollections of Mary Hobson stirred his blood and refreshed his soul. Refreshing was most certainly the word for Mary Hobson—refreshing and exciting and delicious. The previous night's entertainment had been a delight from beginning to end, a magnificent experiment in magnificent debauchery from start to finish, a blessed night from the moment Mary Hobson walked into his house to the moment she was carried out of it.

An experience.

And, at the same time, a cause for alarm.

Because for the first time Dean Hanson had taken a girl at a Unicorn meeting against her will, had banged the bejesus out of a wild wench who, when she walked into his house, had no idea she was going to get the bejesus banged out of her. The others—all the other Unicornettes—had known full well what they were getting into or, more correctly, what was getting into them.

Not Mary Hobson.

She hadn't put up any fight, of course. Far from it. She had been more passionate than anything he could remember in his lifetime, passionate and hot to go and adept at it. But the Mexican Love Potion was the cause of that, and he knew damned well that without it Mary Hobson would be as virginal now as she had been at birth and his basement floor would not be stained with her blood.

He had fed each new member the love potion. But with the others the dosage had been considerably smaller and the potion had been used to increase appetite rather than to produce it. And this made *L'Affaire* Hobson nothing short of rape, pure and simple.

This made it more exciting. If you were going to be depraved, he thought to himself, you might as well go all the way. A hedonist with scruples is a hedonist no longer, and a man who would stop at rape is an insult to the whole concept of depravity.

And so the rape of Mary Hobson had been a rare pleasure, a true treat, a happy experience all around.

But a dangerous one.

That, he thought, was the hell of it. Running a group on the lines of the Unicorns was not comparable to running a Boy Scout troop to begin with, and it was dangerous enough when all the members were willing ones. When you started bringing the innocent ones around and screwing them when they weren't looking you were asking for trouble. And when you asked for trouble you usually got precisely what you asked for.

He stubbed out his cigarette and took the butt from the holder. Carefully he reviewed his position. All in all he wasn't out too far on a limb. Mary could take no action without bringing herself quite prominently into the limelight and could hardly play the outraged rape victim to the hilt. The pictures he had of her with her face contorted in an expression of girlish glee hardly would jibe with such a story. No jury of his peers could look at a cute set of eight-by-ten blowups of little miss Mary busy being banged without strongly suspecting that she wasn't quite so innocent as she pretended to be.

If she was willing to chance her own exposure in order to expose him and the rest of the Unicorns . . . well, that was a chance he had to take. Hell, it was a chance he had already taken. He could only wait and hope for the best, and he could only wait and wish for another crack at the charming charms of Mary Hobson.

The memory of her warmed him again. It would be nice, he mused, if she reacted favorably to the experience. It would be nice if she joined the club as a member in good standing; then he could have another fling at her and see what she was like when she knew what she was doing. He suspected that she would be excellent at it.

She had been good without knowing what she was doing, and she would certainly improve with practice. In addition, she had the edge in appearance on any of the other young things. Looks,

Hanson, realized, were vastly overrated as far as sex was concerned. One rarely saw a girl's face while making love to her and hardly ever saw her figure. Enough flesh on her bones to make a comfortable cushion and enough attractiveness to avoid repelling a man was really all that the sport demanded of a participant. Still, it never hurt if a girl was good looking. And Mary Hobson was certainly good looking.

Hanson smiled to himself. Whatever would happen would happen. Time and time alone would tell whether Mary Hobson wanted his body on hers or his head on a pikestaff. Time would tell, and he could wait in silence for time to clue him in on the state of affairs.

He got up, relaxed now, and ready for dinner. He ate out every evening at the Red Coach Inn on Charter Drive where the best food in Palmer was cooked surprisingly well. Hanson could have afforded a woman to keep house and cook for him, but his chosen pursuits demanded as much privacy as possible. He had a woman come in three times a week to clean all of the house but the basement, which he cared for himself. It was worth eating out to avoid any intrusion on his privacy.

It was dinner time; he was hungry. He headed for the door and had it halfway open before the telephone rang, and when he heard it ring discordantly his first impulse was to let it ring until the cows came home. But something changed his mind and he answered it.

"Is this Dean Hanson?"

"It is."

"I have to see you."

The voice sounded urgent.

"I'm just on my way to dinner," he hedged. "Maybe later this evening—"

"I have to see you right away."

He heaved a sigh. "Well," he said, "I suppose my dinner can wait. Will you come here or what?"

"I'll be right over."

Hanson replaced the receiver and lowered himself once again into his chair. He picked up the cigarette holder, eyed it distractedly, fitted it with a cigarette and got the cigarette going. He smoked slowly and thoughtfully, waiting for the caller to arrive.

His dinner hour was interrupted now and he hated interruptions in what was a pleasant routine. But he wasn't as annoyed as he might have been because the caller promised to be, at the very least, interesting. It would be quite fascinating to find out what all this was all about.

The caller, of course, was Mary Hobson.

And Dean Hanson did not know whether he was going to be threatened, blackmailed, or taken to bed.

Chapter 13

Ed Bainbridge was furious. His muscles were tense as fine-drawn wires and his nerves were shot to hell. He wanted to walk up and down the street and kick the houses over as he passed them.

The dirty bitch.

He still couldn't believe it. Not Mary, not Mary Hobson, not the sweet and pure and beautiful girl he was in love with. Not Mary, not her mixed up with those goddamned Unicorns, not her doing it with God-help-her eight of them, not her, not her, not her . . .

The filthy whore.

The memory of the scene they had had was alive in his head and he couldn't get rid of it. The feeling of shock when she first told him, spilling the words out in a rush one after the other while he stood still in his tracks with his mouth open and his arms hanging at his sides like meat hanging in a butcher shop. The words soaking in and the rage and fury mounting within him as no emotion had ever raced through him before.

The agony that each word and phrase from her lips had brought him. The quick replacement of hurt with hate and pain with rage. The way he had pressed for details, making her tell him everything, making her admit that she had enjoyed every minute of it, that she had sneaked off to the meeting without telling him, making her tell him everything and letting everything that she told him make him angrier and more furious with her.

Until he hit her.

He could still feel the blow, still sense the contact of his open palm with her cheek, still feel the vibrations running up and down the length of his arm from the force of the blow.

She had reeled back. The slap had caught her by surprise and almost knocked her to the ground but somehow she remained standing. She hadn't cried, hadn't whimpered, hadn't registered any emotion whatsoever although God alone knew what might have been going through her mind at the time.

And then he had said, very slowly and very levelly: "As far as I'm concerned you're a dirty slut and I never want to see you again. You can rot in hell forever for all I care about you."

She hadn't said a word and her face had shown nothing at all of what she might have been feeling. She stood, looked at him for perhaps ten seconds, and then turned and walked away from him. He remained where he was for just a few seconds. He watched her, then he turned away and began walking in the opposite direction.

Nobody was any goddamn good. Nobody was decent. Not even a girl like Mary. Mary was a tramp and everybody in the whole damned school was a tramp and to hell with every last one of them.

Everybody was doing it.

Everybody's doing it
Doing what?
Turkey Trot . . .
Turkey Trot

Hot to trot
Got to trot
Gotta get hot
Why not?
Why not?
Why not?

He didn't know where he was going. He was walking, walking fast, thinking fast without thinking anything in particular, silly songs running through his mind and his feet beating a rigid tattoo on the pavement.

And he didn't know where he was going.

But his feet did. His feet knew every step of the way, down Ridgewood Avenue to Leicester, down Leicester to Parkwell, over Parkwell to Cheltenham, along Cheltenham to Essex and down Essex as far as number 119. 119 Essex Street.

A trim little house, brick-and-frame, a three-bedroom plan, well-built, its lawn nicely tended, a deep backyard and a fresh paint job on the house itself.

119 Essex Street.

Bonnie Leigh's house.

How had he known where her house was? When had he been there last, when had he been there at all for that matter? How had his feet found the place, especially in view of the fact that his brain had issued no directive to them?

He didn't know. He hadn't known that he wanted to go to Bonnie Leigh's house.

But the feet knew.

The feet, in all their infinite wisdom, had carried him to the only logical destination. The feet took him where he belonged and now he was standing in front of 119 Essex Street, in front of the brick-and-frame house where Bonnie Leigh lived and loved and lusted.

That was where he belonged. The feet were no dumbbells. They knew what was happening, all right.

Everybody was doing it. Everybody was doing it and it was high time Ed Bainbridge got into the act. High time he knocked off something of his own.

Why not?

Why not?

Here was a girl who was willing. And he thought of a book he had seen on a drugstore rack entitled *All The Girls Were Willing*. A provocative title, to say the least. Well, maybe all the girls weren't willing, but the one at 119 Essex Street sure as hell was, and opportunity was knocking at the door so he might as well open the door in a hurry. Bonnie was there, Bonnie was hot for him, Bonnie was warm for his form, so why in the goddamned name of hell shouldn't he take her up on it?

Why not?

Why not? He rang the bell. To be precise, he leaned on the bell, leaned on it good and hard and didn't let up on it until the door was open and Bonnie Leigh, hot little rabbit-habit Bonnie Leigh was standing there looking sexy with a lay-me smile on her pretty face.

He looked ridiculous, his face so stern, his body so rigid and unbending. She almost laughed but instead held the laughter back and bowed low, a sweeping bow that was properly ludicrous.

"Enter," she said. "Welcome to my humble abode."

He walked in. She closed the door behind him and looked up at him. She wasn't wearing shoes and this made him seem even taller than he actually was in comparison.

"Good afternoon," she said. "You wound up here sooner than I figured. I guessed you'd be around tomorrow or the next day but I didn't expect you this soon. It's quite a tribute to my celebrated appeal."

He still didn't say anything. He stood looking like the great stone face in that story they made you read in first year English and he didn't talk and didn't move and didn't even look especially interested. It was enough to get a girl down.

"Well," she said brightly, "why don't you and I head upstairs?"

She led the way; he followed. She wished he would do something—touch her, try to kiss her, say *something* to her for God's sake. But by the time they reached the head of the staircase she found herself taking a mildly sadistic pleasure in his embarrassment and awkwardness.

This, she decided, was going to be fun. This was going to be an enormous amount of fun—he was *so* shy and *so* ashamed of himself that it was going to be a real blast from beginning to end.

"My bedroom," she said with a flourish.

They entered her bedroom, a small room decorated in a chintzy pattern which Mrs. Leigh thought charming and which Bonnie thought asinine. It always gave her a malicious feeling of glee to copulate furiously in such a prim and proper room.

"My bed," she announced with another flourish.

He looked at the bed. He looked at her again. He looked sick to his stomach.

"My God," she said with another flourish. "Come here, will you? I'm not going to eat you, for goodness sake."

He came closer to her and she let him take her into his arms. It was like being hugged by an oyster without a shell, she thought privately, but she pressed up against him and rubbed her hips against him and got a strange sort of pleasure from the whole thing, from his foolishness and awkwardness and shyness.

She pushed him away.

"Take off your clothes," she suggested.

He stood still and looked stupid.

"Take off your clothes," she repeated patiently. "It's possible with your clothes on but it's a lot better without them. Now if you take your clothes off and I take my clothes off we'll have a lot more fun than if you keep standing there like an idiot."

He seemed a little more alive now. He undressed quickly and she did the same, peeling her clothes off and dropping them on the floor. He stepped out of his pants and looked around vaguely for something to hang them on. She took them from him and dropped them on the floor.

"What the hell," she said, "so you have to press them. Don't worry about it now."

He turned and looked at her, looked at all her bare flesh, looked at her young breasts and slightly curved belly and small behind, and for the first time he showed some genuine signs of life. Without any prompting he took her in his arms and kissed her.

She returned the kiss savagely, impatient now, anxious for it to begin, hungry to get the show on the road. He followed her lead and they tumbled to the bed, their bodies pressed close together and his hands warm on her cool flesh.

He handled her breasts, her thighs, and while his touch was amateurish there was a tremendous excitement in it for her, a real kick that made her desperate for it to start in earnest. She hauled him on top of her and threw back her head and closed her eyes tight and then, all at once, he lay limp in her arms with his head buried in her breasts.

"Hey—"

"I . . . can't," he said.

She sighed. "Of course you can," she said. "Of course you can." And she touched him, and she did the right things to him and for him, and then, miraculously and fortunately, he could.

"Here," she said, supplying him thoughtfully with a contraceptive. "No sense in having any little dividends."

She even had to put the damned thing on for him, for God's sake, but then it began and it was good, quite good, except that it was over much too soon for her and she was left high if not dry.

He started to roll away from her. There was a far-away look in his eyes and a funny expression on his face.

"Hang on," she said, pulling him back with eager hands. "You're not going so soon. Stick around awhile."

He gaped at her.

"Honey boy," she said. "Believe me, it'll be better the second time. You were lousy the first time but that was because it was the first time. It'll be loads better this time."

And she was right. It was.

CHAPTER 14

She was not embarrassed with Hanson. Not at all embarrassed, and this in spite of the fact that he had been the first with her, that he had seen everything that she had done and had taken a hand in everything that had been done to her. But somehow his presence did not disconcert her in the least. He himself was so low, so perverted, that she could not feel personally ashamed of herself when she was with him.

"So that's the way it is," she was saying now. "Ed knows and now he won't have anything to do with me. I don't know what to do."

Hanson was silent. His eyes were studying her intently and she could almost see the wheels turning inside his long and narrow head. He ran one hand through his long hair and said nothing.

"I'm mixed up," she went on, fighting the silence that hung like fog in the room. "It's all over with Ed and I don't know what to do."

"There's no problem."

She looked at him questioningly.

"No problem at all. As I see it, there is only one course open to you."

"What do you mean?"

"It's elementary. You've crossed a bridge and the bridge has caved in behind you. You have to remain on the side to which you've crossed."

"I don't get it."

He raised his eyebrows. "Don't you? It's rather simple. You've been converted to a life considerably different from what you've previously endured. A better life, although you probably don't think of it as such at the moment. But you can take my word that it's a better life."

She shrugged. She felt like asking what was so great about it but she waited for him to explain.

"Look at it this way," he suggested. "At twelve or thirteen years of age Nature outfitted you with the wherewithal for sexual activity. The hormones went into production and the glands grew. Then, after Nature supplied the equipment, Society instructed you to keep the equipment in mothballs for seven or eight years."

"How do you mean?"

"Mary," he said patiently, "for quite a good long while now you've been a desperately frustrated little girl. I'm not singling you out by this designation—a good ninety-five percent of America's adolescents are desperately frustrated. They're physically capable of functioning sexually and Society has imposed an injunction against any sexual experimentation on their part. They are expected to sublimate—either to burn up their energy in sports or studies or to stock up on guilt feelings by secretly masturbating. You've masturbated, haven't you?"

She felt herself blushing.

"Don't be ashamed of it," he said. "It's a virtually universal phenomenon and hardly a cause for shame. The shame of it is that you were forced to seek such an outlet for your sex drive when a far more satisfactory outlet was yours for the taking."

"What's that?"

"What you did last night, simply enough. Right now you think that what you did was wrong. It's natural for you to think that way—seventeen years of societal teaching has an effect that has to be torn up by the roots. In time you'll come to see that everything that you did last night and everything you do in the future is not Bad but Good, not Wrong but Right. If it were not right you would not have wanted it in the first place, you know."

She thought about what he said. Maybe he was telling her the truth, maybe he was right and what she had always been taught was entirely wrong. It was very confusing.

"But . . . all those kids, all together in one room and that movie and—"

"Of course," he said. "That's another of Society's precepts: that sex must be a private thing or it becomes wrong. Privacy is certainly not without its advantages and I won't dispute that. But at times human beings want more than privacy. At times the more orgiastic crowd behavior fills a definite and legitimate human need. Tell me the truth—wasn't the fact that people were watching you while you made love exciting in and of itself? Didn't you get a special sort of pleasure from being observed?"

She thought for a moment. Then she had to admit that he was right, that the presence of the others in the room had only served to intensify her excitement.

"Naturally," he said. "You wanted it, it excited you, and therefore it was valuable. This is not to suggest that you won't prefer privacy at times, but you'll also learn to prefer occasional mob scenes, as it were. By the same token the movie fulfilled a function. You found it sexually stimulating, didn't you?"

"How could I help it?"

He smiled. "Precisely. For that reason you think of it as a *bad* movie, while if you reverse your value system and count as bad that which produces bad results and good what produces good results, you have to acknowledge that the movie was, obviously, a good movie. You enjoyed it, it excited you—what more should a movie do?"

"I—"

"Look," he went on. "Suppose you watch a love story at the local movie house. If it touches your emotions you call it a better picture than if it leaves you cold. Right?"

"Right."

"And suppose it arouses you. Have you ever been aroused while watching a movie?"

"Sometimes," she admitted. "During the love scenes."

"How do you feel at those times?"

She closed her eyes and thought about it. "When they kiss," she said, "it makes me want to . . . kiss."

"That's normal. Now, when you saw the movie last night, how did it make you feel?"

"It excited me."

"It made you want to do what they were doing. Isn't that about it?"

"I guess so."

"So the movie is much the same as the love stories shown openly, wouldn't you say? The difference is a matter of degree. In one they stop at kisses or, at the best, hint that more than kisses is going on off-camera. Outside of that there's relatively little difference."

She had never thought of it that way before. "I guess you're right."

He took a breath, released it, and reached for his cigarette holder, fitting it with a cigarette and lighting the cigarette with his lighter. He offered her a cigarette but she shook her head and he put the pack back on the table next to him.

"Now," he said. "You've said that you don't know what to do. What I'm attempting to explain to you is that what you ought to do is accept full membership in the Unicorns. To do otherwise would be foolish if not impossible. You are a virgin no longer. If you attempt to eliminate sex from your life at this stage, your life will be considerably more frustration filled than it was before you lost your virginity on the field of dishonor. Do you think that after last night, you could go another several years without having a man make love to you?"

"I don't know."

"It wouldn't be easy, would it?"

"I suppose not."

"Well," he said. "you may rest assured that it would not be easy at all. Nor would it be right. So, as I see it, you have two choices. You can join the Unicorns and let your body enjoy the pleasure which is its natural right, or you can live through several years of frustration until you succeed in marrying a boy who has been as frustrated as you have been.

"And any marriage you would make under those conditions wouldn't have much chance of success. You'd marry more for sexual freedom than anything else and the boy would probably be similarly motivated. You wouldn't think so at the time, you'd both call it love but it would all boil down to much the same thing."

"You make the choice sound pretty obvious."

"That's because it is pretty obvious." He smiled and flicked the ash from his cigarette. You've already passed your initiation, you know. Membership is yours; all you have to do is acknowledge it. Along with providing you with a better life, it will kill the guilt feelings which must be plaguing you at present. You'll be able to relax."

She nodded slowly. It would be good to be able to relax, good to stop worrying and stop hating herself, good to let her body do whatever her body wanted to do without having a fistfight with her mind before and after. But something still didn't set right with her. She was a little bit afraid to mention it but it worried her and she had to ask Hanson about it, as much for confirmation of her own right to worry about it as for anything else.

"There's one thing—" she began.

"Go ahead."

"You'll think I'm silly."

"Perhaps. But tell me anyway. If you've got something on your mind you ought to talk about it."

"You'll laugh at me."

"No," he said seriously. "No, I promise you that I won't laugh at you."

"All right," she said. "It's just that . . . well, no matter how good you make it sound and everything, well, I just can't help thinking that it's sinful."

He did not laugh.

"No," he said gently. "No, I'm hardly one to laugh. And I'll have to admit that I know very little about sin. My ancestors, good god-fearing puritans that they were, seemed to know everything there was to know on the subject. I can only assure you that it is not sinful to me and that in time it will not seem at all sinful to you."

She nodded thoughtfully.

"Because," Hanson said, "there is only one sin."

"What is it?"

"Self-denial," Hanson said. "That's the only sin there is in the world."

Suddenly he ground out his cigarette in the big black ashtray with surprising vehemence. Then he stood up just as suddenly and smiled down at her.

"Speaking of self-denial," he said, "I've been denying myself dinner for too long. Since it won't do for us to be seen together, and since it's quite probable that your mother expects you for dinner, I think you ought to be heading for home."

She got up.

"I'll be finished with dinner in approximately an hour, give or take ten minutes. I'll expect you back here shortly thereafter."

Her mouth dropped open as if her jaw had come unhinged. "What for?"

"So that we can make love," he said. "You want me to make love to you, don't you?"

"Yes," she said. And the sound of her own voice surprised her.

"Of course you do," he said. "And I want to make love to you. Last night was certainly charming in its own way but, as I said before, privacy is not without its own sort of merits. You don't have school tomorrow, do you?"

"No—tomorrow's Saturday."

"Fine. Come back here in an hour or so and I'll teach you a few of the things you haven't learned yet. I suspect you'll find the lesson an enjoyable one."

"All right."

He showed her to the door and she walked out and down the walk to the street. Her emotions were all jumbled and she wasn't sure just how she felt. Relief was present, a huge dose of relief at finally being pointed in a definite direction. Fear tempered the relief, guilt seasoned it, and the resultant mixture was a strange one by all counts.

At least she had come to a decision. For better or for worse the die was cast and she didn't have to torture herself any longer.

She smiled to herself. It was the second decision in the one day—the first one had been to tell Ed and that had left her more mixed up than before. But even so, even with Ed reacting as he had reacted, it was far better that she had told him. The two of them were obviously unsuited for each other—he was meant for the world of clean-living God-fearing souls and she was meant for the world populated by people like Dean Hanson. Whichever world was Right, she and Ed did not belong in the same one.

She hurried home, watching the day die around her and the sky darken. There were clouds to the north and she wondered whether it would rain that night. She hoped that it wouldn't. It would be a shame if such a beautiful day was followed by a storm.

But it would be logical, she had to admit. Because the weather was precisely the reverse of her own state of mind. When the sun had blazed down on her and when the sky had been blue and cloudless her own mind had been clouded and her own life uncertain. Now, with the day ending and a storm on the way, now the clouds were lifting from her own existence and a brave new day was dawning.

Chapter 15

According to the rules of the game, Ed Bainbridge had become a man.

That was what the books said. One day you were a boy and the next day you were a man. A girl or woman was what made the difference. The two of you got together at some time in your young life, on a bed or in the back seat of a car or on top of a blanket in Haversham Park, and the two of you squirmed around until a miraculous transformation was somehow affected. At that point you ceased to be a boy and became a man.

Thus Ed Bainbridge was a man.

But he couldn't help feeling that he himself had had relatively little to do with it. At no point had the decision been his. From the point where Mary's disclosure followed close upon the heels of Bonnie's invitation the rest had been inevitable. He couldn't help going to Bonnie's house then, and once he got there she took the lead. In a sense he hadn't made love to her—she had made love to him. The first time, especially, there wasn't much effort required on his part.

But, damn it, he did feel different. And, damn it again, it felt good. And damn it a third time, damn it all the way to hell this time, Old Sobersides Bainbridge was a thing of the past.

He was home now in his own room. He had finished dinner;

now, theoretically, he was doing homework. But his books lay un-opened on the top of his desk and for all he cared they could stay there until the dust on top of them was an inch thick. They could rot as far as he was concerned.

It was Friday night. In another minute or so his father would wander into his room and ask him when he was going to pick up Mary and take her to the show. Every Friday night since the cre-ation of the earth he and Mary had gone to the show. Well, damn it a fourth time, this was one Friday night when he was most defi-nitely not going to the show, one of what would be a long and glorious chain of Friday nights without seeing the goddamned movies at the goddamned movie house.

And, of course, one of a glorious chain of Friday nights when he would not be seeing Mary Hobson. Oh, he might see her again. Someday, if she got lucky, maybe he would be so good as to throw her a piece. Someday, when he ran out of other women to carry off to bed, then perhaps he would give Mary the lucky chance of finding out what a wonderful lover he was. Maybe . . . but not for awhile.

Because he would be playing the field now and there was a lot of territory to play around with. There was plenty of stuff there for you and all you had to do was grab some of it for yourself. Plenty of nice hot little girls with nice bodies and empty heads.

And there would be one hell of a long and glorious chain of them. If all the girls he planned on having were laid end to end it would be a pleasure.

He'd have to hurry, he thought happily. By the middle of June school would be out and he'd have no more cracks at the fleshpots of Palmer. If he took Mr. Schwerner's advice and went to one of the colleges the teacher had suggested, there would undoubtedly be a whole host of serviceable women there to make his life worthwhile. And if, instead, he went to Harvard or Princeton or Yale, there would still no doubt be new fields to conquer.

He studied himself in the mirror. Not bad, he told himself. Good enough, at any rate, to get Bonnie Leigh hot to go. Not that it was any great accomplishment to get a girl like Bonnie ready for bed. The girl must have been born with an itch.

But she did the job well enough, that was for sure. He grinned at his reflection in the mirror. Hell, he was hardly qualified to judge Bonnie's performance on the basis of one afternoon in bed. It wasn't as if he was an expert by any stretch of the imagination.

Well, practice makes perfect.

What he needed was practice.

He got out of the clothes he was wearing and whistled soundlessly as he dressed, selecting a pair of light grey flannel slacks, a striped dress shirt and his blue blazer. He checked himself in the mirror, decided that he looked sharp enough, and left the room.

The telephone was downstairs in the hallway. He lifted the receiver to his ear and dialed a number. A girl answered.

"Anne? This is Ed Bainbridge."

"Ed?"

"Yeah," he said, awkward and hating himself for his awkwardness. "Ed Bainbridge."

"Oh," Anne Kessler said. "Well—"

"I was wondering if you were free tonight."

"Oh," Anne said. It seemed as though it was her favorite word.

"We could go out for a ride," he suggested.

"Oh," she said again. "I thought you were going with Mary Hobson."

"I was."

"Oh," she said. "So that's how it is."

"That's how it is."

"I'm sorry to hear that, Ed."

"Don't be—I'm not."

"Oh," she said. "Well—"

"Be ready in ten minutes," he snapped. "I'll pick you up."

He hung up before she had a chance to say anything and headed for his room again. On the way his father stopped him.

"Not going with Mary tonight?"

"Nope."

"Well," Mr. Bainbridge said. "You know, I'm glad to hear that. Does a kid your age good to play the field a little more. You go with one girl all the time and you tend to get in deeper than you intended. You start necking and pretty soon necking's not enough for you any more. I'm glad to see you spreading out a little."

"That's the way I feel about it, Dad."

Bainbridge nodded. "Makes good sense, Ed. Say, there's nothing wrong between you and Mary, is there? I mean, she's a nice girl and all. I hope there's no broken hearts involved on either side of the fence."

"Oh, no," Ed said. "Everything's fine, Dad."

He smiled softly, went upstairs for his wallet, then came down and got the keys to the family car from his father. He had to hurry. He had told Anne ten minutes and he really had to move if he was going to get to that drugstore on the other side of town first and still meet her on time.

•   •   •

Dean Hanson had a nice bedroom. His bed was huge, one that would accommodate four people comfortably—and probably had, she thought dreamily. The walls were painted a soft yellow-green and soft indirect lighting illuminated them. The carpet underfoot was an inch thick, the desk and dresser and chairs were well-worked mahogany.

And the bed was comfortable. Very comfortable, with both an innerspring mattress and a full box spring to absorb the force of the activity for which the bed was frequently the setting.

That, she thought, was important. If she was going to get laid on a bed it certainly ought to be a good, comfortable bed.

She undressed slowly. Last night she had had help removing her clothes but tonight she was on her own. Hanson wasn't even in the room.

When she was naked she stretched out on top of the bed. She was a little nervous but she smothered the nervousness forcibly and made herself lie still, as close to relaxation as was possible for her. While she was lying there a switch was flipped someplace and the lights in the room dimmed considerably. Then another switch was flipped and soft ethereal music seemed to flow from the walls. There were hidden speakers placed on each wall and the effect was one of complete envelopment in music.

A door opened. Hanson appeared, naked, and she looked at him with interest. He came closer to her, sat down on the edge of the bed and smiled at her.

His mouth found hers. They kissed and his body came down

on hers, his hands squeezing her shoulders and hurting her, his body hard and tense and urgent against her.

She was very much afraid at first. For the first several minutes his caresses frightened her instead of arousing her and her response consisted of muscular tension and an urge to shriek her lungs out.

But then his hands were touching her everywhere and his voice was repeating her name in a tone that was softer than snow. Then the fear drained out of her like dirty water from a bathtub with the plug pulled. Then her muscles relaxed at first and then grew tense again with a tension that was entirely different from the tension of fear.

She needed him now. Her arms engulfed him and her thighs surrounded him and her hungry demanding body surged upward to receive him.

It was as if someone, some giant with tremendous hands, some monster, had taken the world in one fist and was swinging it up and down, back and forth, around and around. That was how it was. The world was swaying like sixty and the music roared and screamed madly and her passion caught her up and held her in a death grip, churning her and spinning her and turning her inside-out and upside-down.

It lasted forever, forever and a day, forever and a week and a month and a year. It was wonderful, it was perfect and from pure perfection it began inexplicably to get still better. It got better and better and better and better and better and then the whole mad wild insane world simply wrapped itself up into a little ball and, with green and blue sparks flying, exploded into little bits and pieces.

Better.

Better.

Better.

Better . . .

Then the explosion. And they lay like rotting logs, drowning in the gentle whirlpool of their own sticky perspiration.

"Do you still think it's a sin?"

Without opening her eyes she knew that he was smiling, that he was looking down at her with a gentle smile on his face.

With her eyes closed she murmured: "Nothing that good is a sin."

She hardly recognized her own voice.

"You enjoyed it?"

"Couldn't you tell?"

"I was just asking."

"Of course I enjoyed it."

"Tell me about it," he said. "Tell me how good it was and how it made you feel."

"Why?"

"I want to hear."

She told him. While she told him, while she spoke softly to him and told him what he had done to her and what she had felt while he did it, his hands were busy on her body and her passion was mounting swiftly.

And so he took her a second time. Quickly now, short and sweet with pain at the beginning and pain at the end, pain that tried to swim in an ocean of pleasure and that was finally drowned by the pleasure. He rolled away from her when it was over and she lay still, unable to move, her breasts aching and her thighs bruised where he had clawed her.

"Sleep," he told her. "It's early and there's plenty of time before your parents will expect you. I'll wake you when it's time for you to go home."

She didn't have the strength to answer.

"Sleep," he repeated.

Then he was gone. Then the lights went out completely and the music swelled in volume and the bed turned feather-soft and she slept.

"Wake up, Mary."

He was shaking her. Her eyes opened after an eternity or two and she looked up at him questioningly.

"Time to get ready for the trip home," he said. "It's almost eleven. Get washed and dressed and I'll give you a ride home."

"Okay."

She slipped out of bed and let him point her to the bathroom. He gave her a towel and she washed and dried herself quickly, then returned to the bedroom and dressed. When she had finished dressing she followed him downstairs to the living room and sat watching him while he smoked a cigarette.

"I had a call while you were sleeping," he said. "We're getting a new member Thursday."

"Who."

"A friend of yours. Bonnie called and said he'd be joining."

"Who is it?"

"Ed Bainbridge."

She couldn't believe it.

But when he told her what Bonnie had told him over the phone she believed it. In a strange way it almost made sense—he evidently rushed straight over to her house, more as revenge on Mary than anything else. What she had told him had obviously come as quite a shock to him and making love to Bonnie was his reaction to the shock.

But it was still hard to believe.

"He'll be initiated Thursday?"

Hanson nodded.

"Dean, is the initiation different for a boy or is it the same as I had?"

Hanson smiled. "Pretty much the same," he said. "It follows the usual pattern—a heavy dose of sexual stimulation from all sides followed by an equally heavy dose of sexual activity. Naturally there's a difference. A man is more depleted physically by large doses of sex. But the principle is much the same."

"I want to deplete him, Dean."

He smiled.

"I mean it," she said. "I have . . . something to settle with him. I want a crack at him, Dean. Okay?"

"Of course," he said. "Whatever you want."

He drove her home, letting her off a few doors away so that no one would notice the car and connect the two of them. She waited while he drove off, the sleek Lincoln racing down the street and taking the corner with wheels screeching. Then she took a deep breath and started along the walk to her house.

It had been a day to remember—one hell of a day, as Bonnie

would probably put it. She had to adjust her whole way of thinking now—Bonnie, who was first a friend and then a betrayer, was now a friend again. Ed, who was first a boyfriend and then an ex-boyfriend, was now an enemy on the same side of the fence she was on. Dean, who was first an unknown and then a perverted tormentor, was now her initiator into the boudoir arts.

It was all very confusing.

But it was easier now, much easier. Her mind was free and her breasts sore and her loins happy as she walked into her house and up the stairs to her room.

Chapter 16

The first things you noticed about Anne Kessler, Ed decided, were her breasts. As a matter of fact, he thought, she could dye her red hair green and paint her rear blue and her breasts would still be the first things you would notice.

They were very noticeable.

It wasn't just the size exactly. It was more than that. It was the way they jumped out at you as if they were going to grab your hands instead of it being the other way around. It was the way they pushed a sweater all out of shape. The sweater in question was a white sweater, and a sweater that was not really the same size as Anne Kessler was, and the ultimate result of all this was that you could see those breasts almost as clearly as if their owner were not wearing a sweater.

The fact that it was a white sweater was significant. Because of this, you could see right through the silly thing, see the darker skin at the tips, see the way the nipples jutted out so nicely.

And they were *so* big.

Bigger than Bonnie's, which wasn't much of a test. Bigger than Mary's, which was. So damned big, and so damned nice, and you could see them almost as clearly as if she wasn't wearing a sweater at all.

Which, he told himself firmly, she wouldn't be in not too long.

"Where are we going?" she asked, inside the car now, sitting close to him but not close enough so that they were touching. He wanted to ask her to sit a little closer, to cuddle up in the car right next to him, but for Christ's sake, they were still in her driveway. There was such a thing as being too cool, for God's sake.

"Nowhere special."

"There's a nice picture at—"

"No," he said, cutting her off. "I don't much feel in the mood for a picture tonight. All the movies are the same."

"Well—"

He backed the car out of the driveway, then started driving slowly along her street. Out of the corner of his eye he studied her, studied the slightly lost expression on her relatively pretty face, studied once more her thoroughly unbelievable mammary development. He wondered whether it would be any different doing it with a girl whose breasts were so big, so exciting to look at. It seemed as though it ought to be, anyhow. Just thinking of all that hot-looking flesh pressed up against his chest was enough to make him squirm around in his seat.

"Just let's go for a drive," he suggested. "We're interesting people, you and me. We won't be at a loss for words, you and me. Or at a loss for things to do. I'm sure we'll make out okay."

He eyed her again, getting a quiet charge out of the way she wasn't sure just what was coming off. Well, he could tell her what was coming off if she really wanted to know. Any minute now that white sweater of hers was coming off, that's what. And when it did he was going to have the time of his life.

"Ed—"

"Yeah?"

"I don't get it. You've always been the straight-arrow type, you know?"

"What do you mean?"

She shrugged. "Oh, you know."

"Nope."

"*You* know."

"Why don't you tell me?"

She shrugged again. "Well," she began hesitantly, "you were always going with Mary. You know."

"So?"

"But—"

"I *was* going with her," he said. "Not any more. I told you that over the phone—we broke up and I'm in circulation again. That's why I called you. So if you think you're breaking something up between the two of us you can forget all about that angle. Mary and I are through, finished, washed up—and I'm glad of it. You're not intruding on someone else's territory if that's what's on your mind."

She grinned and he caught the grin out of the corner of his eye. She was, he decided, a pretty sexy little minx. His speech evidently was only getting her more interested in the whole scene.

"Ed," she told him, "I wouldn't care if I was breaking something up. I'd probably get my kicks out of it, you know? Like I was the evil woman doing the good woman wrong, in the movies and everything."

Christ, he thought, what a dumb little broad. He said: "You—evil? You don't strike me as the evil type, Anne. I don't think you could be evil if you tried."

"No?"

He shook his head, enjoying the role he was playing. He had never used a line before, had never needed one with Mary, but now he was beginning to find out for himself how much fun it can be to feed a lot of baloney to a girl.

"Try me," she breathed. "See how evil I can be. I can be plenty evil, Ed."

He turned left at Three Mile Road, drove a steady 45 miles an hour out past Hogan's Mill to a grove of poplar trees. He kept feeding her the steady line of nonsense all the way, kept sneaking glances at her breasts, and kept on enjoying himself. He wondered if she was going to get coy when he parked the car. He knew damned well that it wouldn't come as any surprise to her, and he knew that she would be pretty disappointed if he didn't get in her pants, but he had a funny feeling she was going to put on a frightened virgin act or something along those lines. If she did, it might be even more fun. He knew he'd win in the end, and the way he felt now he'd rape her if he had to. Yes, damn it, if she forced him to he'd rape her—rip that sweater off and pull that skirt up and tear off those panties and push her down on the seat and give it to her.

His hands, slippery with sweat, had trouble gripping the wheel.

"Ed—"

"Yeah?"

"How come you're driving way out here?"

"Nice scenery," he lied. "I always get a kick out of looking at something nice."

He looked hard at her breasts as he said the last sentence.

Then, deliberately, he raised his eyes until they caught her own eyes and held them.

Then he smiled.

"I know what you mean," she said. "The trees and the sky and everything."

"Yeah," he said. "And the hills. We better not forget about the hills."

And he followed this with another meaningful glance at her breasts.

His mouth was unusually dry, his hands slipperier than ever with perspiration. His head throbbed dully and he couldn't wait much longer. Finally he picked his spot. He cut the motor and eased the big car off the road. Deliberately he yanked up the emergency brake, nudged the gearshift lever into PARK position, and doused the headlights. Then, as if he had arrived at his own home or something, he leaned back into the seat, yawned and stretched.

"Ed," she was saying, "why did you park the car?"

"Huh?"

"You parked."

"Yeah," he said sarcastically. "I guess you might say that's fairly obvious."

"But why?"

"Guess."

She closed her eyes and pretended to be thinking. He moved closer to her and he could feel the heat of her warm body reaching across to him. His fingers itched to hold onto those big breasts of hers but he kept them under control and waited.

He was enjoying this.

And he guessed that he'd enjoy what was coming even more. Lots more.

"You must have the wrong ideas about me," she was saying now. "I bet I know what you're thinking."

"What?"

"Oh," she said cunningly, "I bet you think . . . oh, it's not even nice to talk about it."

"Go ahead."

She considered. "Well," she said, softly, "I have the idea that you think I'm the sort of girl who lets a boy go all the way with her."

"Are you?"

She pretended to be shocked. "Ed," she said, "I'm not that kind of girl. I don't know where you got the idea but it's not true."

"I see," he said.

"I'd never permit anything like that," she went on earnestly. "I'm going to remain a virgin until I'm married. I decided that a long time ago."

"Well," he said, "I suppose that's the only really proper thing to do."

"Of course."

"I never thought you were the type of girl to go all the way anyhow," he lied. "I never had any ideas like that of course."

"That's good," she said. "I'm glad you're the type of boy who wouldn't try to take advantage of a girl."

"I should hope not."

"Some boys are like that," she said. "I'm glad to hear that you're not."

"Perish the thought."

"Of course," she continued, "that doesn't mean I wouldn't let you kiss me if you wanted to."

"Do you think that would be all right?"

"Well," she said, "I think so. Just a few times, of course."

Grinning, they kissed. The first kiss was just a quick peck but the softness of her lips amazed him. Her mouth was so soft, so sweet, and he felt himself getting excited just from that quick kiss.

The second kiss was different. This time his tongue slipped between those soft lips of hers, tasting them, caressing them. At first she kept her teeth shut against him but his tongue caressed her lips and her teeth parted to admit him to the inner recesses of her sweet mouth. His tongue found hers and he could feel the passion churning within her.

But she wasn't like Bonnie. Instead of going all out right away she was trying to master her passion—fighting it, letting it build up bit by bit in preparation for what had to be the ultimate explosion.

He was excited.

They kissed again and this time her tongue was the aggressor, probing the depths of his mouth and making him more and more passionate. He rubbed the small of her back with hot hands, squeezed one shoulder, drew her in tight against him. Now he could feel the softness of her breasts through her sweater and his shirt. He longed to get rid of the sweater and the shirt, to have her tight and warm against his bare skin.

The kiss ended.

"That was nice," she whispered. "I like the way you kiss. And I don't think there's anything improper about it."

"Of course not."

"If you want I'll let you feel me a little. Do you think you'd like that?"

He nodded because he couldn't speak.

"Just a little," she said. "I wouldn't say this to anybody else because they might get the wrong idea. But I think I can trust you."

He nodded and she came to him. When he touched her breast through the thin sweater he couldn't believe anything in the world could feel so good. It was unbelievable, so soft and yet so firm, so big in his big hand.

His hands cupped her breasts, squeezing and relaxing, squeezing and relaxing. She didn't make a sound but he could tell what he was doing to her, that he was driving her out of her mind with pure passion. Her eyes were shut tight and her shoulders were rigid and she was breathing very hard and very fast.

He kept doing it, fondling her breasts, pinching her nipples gently, until he just couldn't take it any more. This was so different than the way it had been with Bonnie. This was slow and gentle, teasingly slow and tantalizingly gentle.

It was good. Very good.

"Ed—"

He was holding her close to him now, his hands around her back. Both of them were breathing very intensely. He heard her say his name but he was unable to answer.

"If you took off my sweater," she said now, "you could touch me better. Would you like to do that? Would you like to touch me without any sweater in the way?"

She raised her arms up over her head and he pulled her white sweater loose from her skirt. With shaking hands he drew the sweater up over her head and off.

At first he could only look.

Her breasts were perfect, so perfect, so absolutely perfect that he could not believe what he was looking at. When he touched her, his hands actually holding that bare and perfect flesh, it was all he could do to keep from screaming.

And she was easily as excited as he was. The only difference was that she was trying to conceal her excitement while there was no way for him to hide his. He discovered things about her, discovered that when he did certain things to her flesh it was more exciting than other things that he did.

She said: "Kiss them."

She did not have to ask him a second time. He pushed her down on the seat and leaned over her, his mouth searching eagerly and hungrily for her breasts.

It was like a dream. Slowly, with a lot of time for every action, he worked on her breasts. He did everything that there was to do.

And she loved it.

"Ed, reach under my skirt."

He reached under her skirt and found paradise. The skin on the inside of her thighs was as soft as the skin on her breasts, maybe even softer, and he touched her there and kissed her breasts all at once.

He removed her flimsy panties without even being asked.

He wanted to take her and he knew that she would not fight him now, that she wanted it and was ready for it. But he wanted to prolong this ecstasy as long as was humanly possible. He was discovering that there was no need to rush and no need to hurry, that the preliminaries themselves were a tremendous source of joy.

He was inventive.

He did many things to her.

Many very interesting things.

Intriguing things.

Things that, a day or two ago, he would have considered disgustingly perverted.

But that was a day or two ago.

Now it was a different story.

He touched everything, kissed everything, and there finally came a point when it was time for it to begin, when to wait longer would have been sheer torture, when it had to commence or they both would have died on the spot.

He took her from the car and spread the blanket he had had the good sense to bring upon the ground. She took off her skirt now and he pulled off all his clothing, tossing his pants inside-out upon the ground.

They fell together to the blanket.

Now, with all of her nude and hot against all of him, it was perfect, the absolute height of physical sensation. Her legs parted for him and her arms went around his back and crushed him to her.

"Ed—"

It began and it was the end of the world, the end of the entire world, the end of anything and of everything. It was perfection, absolute perfection, the essence and quintessence of perfection, and when something is absolutely one hundred percent perfect there is very little else you can say about it other than how perfect it is.

It was perfect.

"Ed!"

Blood beat on his brain and inside his brain. The world took a trip to the moon.

"Ed, make it last forever . . ."

It was a tall order. But, indeed, he came as close as possible to making it last forever. It lasted and lasted and perfection itself kept improving, kept getting still more perfect.

And then she began to chant, and the chant rose in volume to a screaming shriek that they must have heard in Cairo. Over and over she screamed one word, one short word, over and over and over.

It was a simple word, a very ordinary word, but it seemed to sum up everything. At that precise point in time it summed up all of human existence from the beginning of time on to some point in the future. It was, that word, everything that there was to be said on every subject under the sun.

Chapter 17

The boy's name was Dave Winters and he knew something. He knew of the existence of the Unicorns.

Dave Winters was no detective. He was a slight, small-boned boy with limp wheat-colored hair and a scattering of ruby-red pimples on his forehead. He was generally undistinguished in the classroom, out of place on the athletic field, and a complete and total social outcast.

There was nothing outstanding about Dave Winters, nothing memorable, nothing remotely important. Dave Winters, all things considered, was a useless nonentity with the individuality of a Japanese cigarette lighter and the dynamic personality of a cockroach.

But he knew something.

He knew that every Thursday night for several months a group of boys and girls in the senior class of Palmer High School had been meeting at the home of Dean Hanson on State Street. He knew what they did there. And the knowledge burned in his brain like money in a wastrel's pocket.

His knowledge was limited. He had never been a participant, needless to say. Dave Winters the Nonentity was hardly a likely candidate for Unicorn membership. Ruthellen Perkins summed up the situation quite lucidly in a conversation with Bonnie

Leigh when she speculated that Dave Winters was quite possibly the only person alive whom you could sleep with without realizing it. This observation was only idle speculation, of course, because Dave Winters had never slept with Ruthellen Perkins. Dave Winters had never slept with anybody, and quite conceivably never would.

But, because Dave Winters was such a complete nothing, because you could look at him without seeing him, Dave Winters learned things. When Moose Gardens and Jack Lacey were talking in the locker room they didn't lower their voices when Dave Winters approached. They just didn't notice him, or if they did he didn't seem enough of a threat to force them to whisper. When Anne Kessler and Larry Prince were busying themselves with some mild petting and hinting darkly at the pleasure they would give each other come Thursday eve, they did not realize that Dave Winters had blundered within hearing range.

There were many more incidents of a similar nature. Dave Winters was not intelligent enough to catch on until quite a few such incidents had occurred, but once he got the message he began a concerted campaign of dropping the eaves. And before too long a period of time had elapsed, Dave Winters knew something.

Dave Winters was no mental giant. He wasn't much of anything, but he did at least know what you did if you were a person who Knew Something.

You Told Somebody.

Just who to tell was something of a problem. At first he thought of telling his mother, but when he thought it over he decided that it wasn't too good an idea. His mother was a gaunt, hatchet-faced woman with a sharp tongue and beady eyes, and

Dave Winters was confident that if he said anything about the Unicorns to her he would be punished. She would be firmly convinced that he, her errant son, had been deeply and direly involved with the whole thing.

For a few desperate moments Dave Winters passionately wished he were religious. If he were, then he could go tell the whole thing to a priest and get it off his mind. Then the priest would tell him what to do and it wouldn't be his problem any more.

It was quite a mess, and if a solution hadn't popped into Dave Winters' pointed head in due time, it is quite likely that he would have joined the Church in desperation. But finally he came up with a plan. There was, at last, someone he could tell.

The man he selected was Samuel Pierce. Samuel Pierce, in his official capacity of principal of Nathan Palmer High School, seemed at once the obvious man to confide in. The problem was a school problem and Samuel Pierce was the Ultimate School Authority.

Dave Winters went to him with an overwhelming feeling of relief rushing through his system.

Samuel Pierce, as everybody knew, was a busy man. This was common knowledge and might not be worth reporting except for the fact that, common knowledge or not, Samuel Pierce really was not a busy man at all. He simply appeared busy, and had with consummate skill parlayed the appearance of busyness into a respected position in the community, a decent job, and a relatively small and easily handled amount of work.

"I'm very busy today," Pierce told Dave Winters. While this was not at all true it sounded good and Pierce himself actually felt that he was telling the truth. There was a pile of papers on his desk, as it happened, and while these papers had been there for years and would be there for as many more years as Samuel Pierce remained in that office, he would still go through them methodically as soon as Dave Winters said whatever he had to say and left Samuel Pierce to pore over his papers.

"I'm quite busy," he repeated, "so try to make this quick if you can."

Dave Winters nodded, then gulped soundlessly. It was turning out to be more difficult than he had suspected to confide in Samuel Pierce. But he made a supreme effort.

"There's a club," he began.

Samuel Pierce nodded.

"A club," Dave Winters repeated, gaining confidence. "They meet every Thursday night."

"I see," said Samuel Pierce, who didn't really and who wished fervently that the young fool would come to the point.

"They aren't allowed to have clubs," Dave Winters said. "Clubs like that aren't allowed. They have meetings and do things and it isn't right."

"Oh," said Samuel Pierce. "They've started a fraternity, have they? I see."

Fraternities and sororities had been outlawed at Nathan Palmer High School. Before Samuel Pierce had stepped into his job the former principal had realized that such organizations, ridiculous enough on a college campus, were thoroughly absurd on the high school level. He had outlawed them, and while Samuel

Pierce would never have bothered instituting such a regulation, he never troubled to remove it from the books.

"Not exactly a fraternity," Dave Winters said. "Something like that."

"I see," Pierce said. Fraternities and sororities had been cropping up persistently at Palmer during his administration and from time to time various ones came to his attention. Pierce, who derived many of his ideas from an American Secretary of State, ignored the groups in the hope that they would go away, which they invariably did in a short period of time.

"Not a fraternity," Winters persisted annoyingly. "They have boys and girls in it."

"More like a club?"

The boy nodded gratefully. "And they have meetings," he pushed on, "and they have initiations and they go to movies and they do things."

Pierce, who didn't care a hoot for or against movies, initiations and things, nodded sagely. In time, he thought, this idiot boy would go away and leave him alone. Just one master stroke to convince the fool that he was interested ought to do the trick.

Pierce picked up a pencil. "This club," he mused. "What do they call themselves?"

"Unicorns," Dave Winters whispered.

"Unicorns," Samuel Pierce repeated.

"Unicorns," he wrote in neat pencil script on a sheet of paper. He placed the paper on top of the ever-present pile of papers in the middle of his desk.

"I'll look into it," he assured the boy. "You can go now."

Dave Winters departed gratefully, his conscience at peace, his soul at rest, and the burden of his awful knowledge gone forever from his mind. Two days later Samuel Pierce found the slip of paper with *Unicorns* written upon it in the middle of the muddle on his desk. He laughed happily, crumpled the paper into a hard little ball and flipped it into his wastebasket.

Unicorns indeed!

Unicorns indeed.

By the middle of January the Unicorns had settled down into what could be called either a groove or a rut, depending upon your point of view. From the point of view of the members themselves there were no two ways about it. It was a groove, a gas, the end of the entire world. Life was a continual bubble of joy, and only an unmitigated party-pooper could dare to suggest that one of these days the bubble was going to burst.

Individual reaction varied from sheer ecstasy to bland acceptance. Girls like Bonnie Leigh and Ruthellen Perkins, and boys like Jack Lacey and Ray Saltonstall could not have been happier under any circumstances. As far as they were concerned the Messiah had arrived and the golden age had dawned.

The opposite point of view was exemplified by Ed Bainbridge. He was no less exuberant a participant than any of the others, but when he was alone by himself his attitude was considerably different than when he was with the rest of them in Hanson's basement. Alone, with no girls present to arouse him and no movies to divert his attention, Ed had to admit that everything was basically wrong. He couldn't alter his whole way of thought, couldn't force himself to accept as right what he knew was wrong.

But he was in too far to get out. And staying in was far more enjoyable than getting out, even if an escape route should have been opened for him. He was young, after all, and the pleasure that the club afforded him was ample compensation for the mental traumas that hit him from time to time.

Mary Hobson felt much the same way, although for her Hanson's arguments had clouded the moral issue. She knew only that she was happier now, that she slept better at night and that she no longer had to touch herself in secret to quiet the forces that worked within her.

The club as a whole had levelled off on an even keel. Hanson, convinced that he had a good thing and worried that it might slip away from him if he wasn't careful, had imposed several rules and regulations in the interest of security. They were instantly accepted without question by the entire membership.

The rules were simple. First and foremost, Hanson decreed that no new members would be taken into the Unicorns. The club had reached its ideal quota of eighteen members and Hanson was afraid that if it grew any larger detection would become inevitable. While several of the members had their eyes on several non-members whom they thought would make excellent bedmates, Hanson's word was accepted as law. What he had said made good sense.

Another rule which wasn't accepted quite so readily was that sexual activities would be confined strictly to club meetings. Again, this rule was made for security purposes. While the Unicorns enjoyed full privacy in the confines of Hanson's home, such privacy was hard to come by elsewhere in Palmer. There was never any guarantee that a couple in the throes of passion might not be spotted by some outsider, in which event the whole business might come to the attention of the outside world.

A week, as Bonnie Leigh asserted privately to Betty Jo Meltzer, was a long time to wait for a lay, especially when you were used to getting it steadily. But Bonnie didn't break the rules openly. From time to time a male member visited her bedroom, but such visits were kept secret and were the exception rather than the rule.

The meetings themselves were supposed to be the sole source of sexual satisfaction and Hanson spared no effort to make them as exciting and satisfying as possible. Through careful cultivation of his Boston contacts he worked to convert the basement into a sort of Sex Palace. Huge full-color blowups of pornographic pictures were mounted on the walls of the main basement room and the several antechambers as well. A library of obscene books was set up in one of the side rooms and books were loaned out to the members upon request. Hanson had money, a good deal of money, and he could think of no better way to spend it than upon his own physical gratification.

The results were gratifying.

When Dean Hanson presided at a meeting of the Unicorns he felt for all the world like the emperor Nero conducting a Roman orgy. The comparison was not entirely a case of delusions of grandeur. Unicorn meetings were becoming highly developed affairs.

Everybody did everything with everybody. In no time at all every girl had been enjoyed by every boy and pretty soon different individuals began concentrating upon different techniques. With a spirit of youthful zest and zeal, the members worked hard for originality. It was the age of specialization and the Unicorns were not the ones to buck a trend.

Everybody did everything and everybody loved it. By late February the worst of a relatively mild winter had passed and the coming of spring brought a renewed excitement into the proceedings. The group was beginning to realize that there wasn't much time left. Soon June would come and graduation would end their connection with Nathan Palmer High School. What would happen to the Unicorns then was anybody's guess. Slightly over half the membership was college bound, and as a result their contact with the rest would be limited to vacation time. Three of the boys would be stuck in the army for the next two years, with only occasional furloughs to devote to Unicorn activity. Others undoubtedly would move away. By the looks of things the group only had until June before the game would be over.

There was no point in wasting time. March, April, May and June and then it would all be over. As Hanson put it, it was unlikely that they would ever find the same degree of sexual freedom elsewhere. There were other clubs, he told them, clubs for married couples where wife-trading provided a temporary respite from the monotony of monogamy. But, he assured them, they would be hard-pressed to find anything like the Unicorns.

His speech sounded like a parody of a high school valedictorian's address to the graduating class. But what he was saying was certainly true enough. The Unicorns were unique. Their activities constituted a high point or a low point in human behavior, again depending upon your point of view.

Let us look more closely into these activities. Let us examine a meeting, one which is no more or less exotic than the average.

We are in the home of Dean Hanson on State Street. It is a warm night for March in Palmer. March this year has come in not like a lion but like the lamb it is supposed to go out like. The trees are already beginning to spout leaves, the lawns are already green, the days are already mild and the breezes already balmy.

Outside tonight the moon is full in a cloudless sky. Stars dot the blackness of the sky and the wind is gentle in the trees. But we are not outside. We are in Hanson's basement and we are watching a unique and entertaining spectacle.

Pay attention . . .

Chapter 18

Everyone was nude. This simplified things—clothing can be difficult to remove when fingers are clumsy with excitement. But, in spite of their nudity, all the members sat alone, kept their hands to themselves and maintained strict discipline.

Weeks ago this might have been different, but with the passage of time they had grown so accustomed to one another's bodies that nudity in and of itself was no longer a cause for excitement. An air of detached interest filled the room as Hanson walked to the front and prepared to speak.

"Tonight's movie is a good one," he said. "I think you'll find it quite interesting."

"Is it in color?"

Hanson shook his head, and Chuck Folsom, who had asked the question, was disappointed. He had a deep streak of the voyeur in him and enjoyed watching at least as much as actual participation. The two color movies he had seen had made a deep and abiding impression upon him.

"All that remains," Hanson went on, "is the assigning of partners. You may pair off as follows: Dave Carson with Judy Simmons, Marv Gardens with Anne Kessler, Larry Prince with Mary Hobson, Jack Lacey with Bonnie Leigh, Ed Bainbridge with Gladys Kent . . ."

Hanson continued assigning partners, a recent innovation designed to ensure variety. As the names were called the boys and girls paired off and sat together. Hanson himself was paired with Laura Rose and he led the girl to a spot on the floor while he got the projector started.

The house lights went down. The projector whirred. The movie began.

TITLE CARD: GETTING IN SHAPE

Medium shot of a door inscribed "John Hightower's Exercise Parlour." A woman, tall and busty and wearing a skirt and sweater that emphasize her figure approaches the door, then knocks on it. A tall well-built man answers the door. He is wearing a pair of boxer shorts and nothing else.

SUBTITLE: "I WANT TO GET SOME EXERCISE."

Close-up of man's face as he winks at the camera.

SUBTITLE: "YOU CAME TO THE RIGHT PLACE. TAKE OFF YOUR CLOTHES."

The woman dutifully strips down to bra and panties. When the man gestures to indicate that she should remove these garments as well the woman solicits his assistance. He steps up behind her, unhooks and removes her bra, and takes her large breasts in his hands. After a few seconds of breast manipulation the man releases the woman. She steps back and removes her panties as well.

The camera pans slowly, starting with the woman's head and traveling upward to her face. She is smiling vacuously.

SUBTITLE: "WE'LL START OFF WITH SOME PUSH-UPS."

The man does several push-ups to show the woman what is required of her. The woman evidently gets the message and begins doing push-ups herself. The camera focuses on a close-up of her posterior which the man strokes with one hand.

SUBTITLE: "THERE'S A BETTER WAY TO DO IT."

The man removes his boxer shorts. This interests the woman no end and the camera moves for a medium-shot as she examines her discovery. Then the man lies down on his back on the floor.

SUBTITLE: "NOW TRY IT."

The woman positions herself over the man and resumes doing push-ups. After a few seconds of this activity the man and woman make love in this position. The camera work now consists primarily of extreme close-ups of the areas involved with an occasional long shot for contrast.

Moose Gardens was worried. He was sitting beside Anne Kessler, his partner for the evening, and he was quite definitely worried. He was afraid he was going to kill somebody. The thought was not a pleasant one. The thought of committing a murder is rarely a pleasant one, but at the moment it was definitely an exciting one.

This is what worried Moose Gardens.

He was sweating freely and he wiped at his forehead with one hand, telling himself to be calm, to relax, that there was nothing to worry about. But, damn it, there *was* something to worry about. There was plenty to worry about, for Christ's sake.

It was the damnedest thing, the way these urges came over him. He couldn't understand it and he was afraid to think much about it. But he kept having the strangest desires to hurt people, to cause pain, to . . . kill.

Thinking back, he realized that he had always had desires something along those lines. Maybe that was what made him such a good lineman in football; when he went in for a tackle he hit that ball carrier as hard as he could and he got a real kick out of slamming into a guy. That was okay on a football field, but when you started getting impulses like that off the field there was something wrong.

Idly he reached out a hand and cupped Anne's breast. She purred like a kitten and he had an insane wish to squeeze her breast until she yelled her lungs out. His fingers were shaking as he forced himself to release her and dropped his hand to his side.

It was crazy, just plain crazy! Maybe he ought to see a doctor or something, maybe he ought to have his head examined. There had to be some way to stop thinking about things like this.

And those books Hanson had sure didn't help. Books with women getting tortured, books about torture and pain and women screaming, and every time Moose read one of them he would get so edgy and so nervous and so excited that he couldn't stand up, let alone think straight. He knew better than to look at those books, knew what they were doing to him.

But he couldn't stop reading them, couldn't stop thinking terrible thoughts and wishing terrible wishes. His dreams were so vivid some nights that he would wake up with the sweat soaking the sheets beneath him, with fear gripping him like a giant steel hand around the throat.

He watched the movie for a few minutes but that only made matters worse. So, for that matter, did the caresses which Anne Kessler was bestowing upon him. He said a brief prayer and turned to the girl, his hand reaching instinctively for her breast.

He squeezed.

"Ouch! Hey, Moose, that hurt!"

The words were like music. *Gentle now*, he told himself. *That's enough for one night.*

And, gently, he took the girl in his arms.

The man and woman on the screen are tireless. After each has taken a turn at doing push-ups, the two stand up and look at each other.

The man speaks.

SUBTITLE: "NOW SEE IF YOU CAN TOUCH YOUR TOES."

The woman tries to touch her toes. When she bends over in this manner her breasts dangle pendulously and the man takes them in his hands. The woman struggles to touch her toes without success while the man holds onto her large breasts.

SUBTITLE: "KEEP TRYING."

After a few more attempts the woman manages to touch her toes. The man releases her breasts and positions himself behind her. He strokes her buttocks with both hands.

Medium-shot of the two of them in this position.

Close-up of the woman's face.

Brief intercourse scene.

"Mary, let's do it this way."

Mary knew what Larry Prince meant. But, hoping she was wrong, she asked him anyway.

And he told her.

"Please," she said.

"What's the matter?"

"I don't want to."

"Why not?"

"I just don't like it."

"Oh, for Christ's sake!'

"Larry—"

"C'mon, will you?"

"But I don't like it. I really don't, Larry. It makes me feel dirty. It makes me feel like something that just crawled out of the sewer."

"Well?"

She looked at him.

"Look," he said, "just who in hell do you think you are, anyway? You're not the Virgin Mary, you know. Far from it. You don't have to feel so goddamn pure. What have you got to feel pure about?"

It was a good question.

"All right," she said.

"I mean you're no better than anybody else, for God's sake. You're the same as—"

"I said all right. What more do you want from me?"

He showed her.

The movie went on.

And so did the meeting.

Ed Bainbridge and Gladys Kent were lying in each other's arms. They had finished what they were doing. Gladys seemed to be sleeping; Ed had his eyes open but he was not looking at anything.

His mind was not running in the same channels as the other minds in Dean Hanson's basement. It had been, but now that he and Gladys had done what they had come to do he was thinking of something else.

Perhaps it is not entirely correct to say that he was thinking. Actually his brain was tuned in to one simple thought, one unanswerable question that repeated itself again and again and again.

Where was it all going to end?

Chapter 19

Moose Gardens was in a bad way.

Here it was, he thought. The middle of April, the spring of the goddamn year, and where in hell was he? He was in one hell of a mess, that was where he was. Just about every way you looked at it he was in a mess, and he did not like it at all. Not one bit.

School, for instance. Not that he was normally the world's greatest goddamn student to begin with, but it was never like this before. Usually he didn't have any trouble. He did his work regularly and studied as much as he had to and got by.

Not with flying colors, maybe, but not with his tail dragging between his legs either. Some of the better athletes needed a little pressure on the faculty from the coach in order to qualify for sports participation, but he hadn't been in that class. Not him—never on the honor roll but never failing, a nice steady average that never dropped below eighty and never soared above eighty-five. Even keel all the time with no sweat, and for a guy who played three sports and was goddamn good at one of them, this was by no means a bad record.

That's how it used to be, he thought. But that was sure as hell not how it was. Not now.

Not for a good long while.

Not since he started in with the Unicorns.

Since then things had begun taking a steadily downhill plunge. At first he blamed it on football—he worked his head off for the football team and that, obviously, was why the history course was bugging him and why trig functions kept slipping away from his grasp. With the college scouts looking him over and the whole rest of his life depending upon how he looked out there on the goddamn football field, how in hell was a guy supposed to keep up-to-date in his courses?

And during the fall the faculty had been quite understanding. They knew he was the best thing that ever happened to the Palmer team and they were willing to look the other way if he was a day or two late with an assignment or unprepared for a recitation or lower than usual on a quiz.

But swimming didn't take up the time football did. He wasn't that good, for one thing, and practice was less important, for another thing, and swimming in general didn't make that much difference as far as a scholarship was concerned. Just being on the team was important because the colleges liked it if you were active all year round, but he wasn't going to get or lose a scholarship on the strength or weakness of his speed in the water.

And his grades went down.

And his best time in the 100-yard freestyle was twenty seconds slower than his best time the year before.

Now they were playing baseball. *They* were—but he wasn't. First-string first baseman since his second year and now he was off the goddamn team because he couldn't hit and couldn't field and couldn't run.

Old Lagniappe was nice enough about it. Too much football he had called it—too much on the football field had tightened up his goddamn muscles so that he was good for football and nothing else. That, Lagniappe explained, was probably what loused him up in the water. The two sports called for two different sets of muscles and two different types of reflex action, and a good lineman was hardly ever good for much else.

That's what the coach had said.

But Moose knew better.

It was the Unicorns. It was the goddamn Unicorns and the goddamn things they were doing to Moose. And there was no question about it, it was certainly doing things to him. Making him think crazy things, things he never thought about before. Things about hurting and cutting and killing, things about knives and tortures and women and things like that, things that got right into his blood and pounded in his ears and drove him so crazy he couldn't think about anything else. He would sit in classes and not hear a word, turn on the radio and not catch a thing, and when he tried to sleep at night his brain burned and he tossed and turned with the crazy things that were killing him.

Nothing like this had ever happened before, before the goddamn Unicorns got rolling and he got rolling along with them, before the movies and the books and the goddamn girls and girls and girls.

He scratched his head. No, he admitted, he couldn't blame everything on the Unicorns. There had been some things before. Dreams, mostly—dreams about girls and dreams of pain that he couldn't entirely remember. But nothing like now, nothing like now when he couldn't think about anything else.

And it kept getting worse. Now he was doing crazy things, things that didn't make any sense at all. Things that scared the hell out of him, things like carrying a switchblade knife with a seven-inch blade with him wherever he went.

He was sitting in his own living room now and he took the knife from his pocket and pressed the button and watched the steel blade snap into place. Vaguely he tried to remember how the knife had come into his possession. He'd had it for years, he remembered, had acquired it in one of those trades that went on endlessly when you were a kid in grade school. It probably had cost him two frogs and an autographed baseball at the time—he was damned if he could remember.

Then they passed a law making switch knives illegal, and in a proper law-abiding fashion he packed the knife away and put it in a carton in the cellar. There it remained, almost but not quite gone, almost but not quite forgotten.

Until two weeks ago, when some hidden impulse caught up with him when he was down in the cellar to get a steak from the freezer for his mother. Some impulse made him go to the carton, open it, rummage around in it, find the knife and pop it into his pocket.

He had not put it back. Instead he carried it with him constantly and put it methodically beneath the mattress as he slept, as if he had to keep it near him, as if somebody would try to take it from him unless he was ultra-careful with it.

Lots of times he would take out the knife and look at it, would polish the keen steel until it made a mirror for his own fierce eyes, until it was as sharp as a razor, sharp enough so that he could shave the hairs on the backs of his hands with it.

He looked at the knife now, peered at his reflected image, and his brain filled up with pictures of himself and the knife and a nameless and faceless girl. The crazy things were horrible, sickening, the worst things in the world.

His ears were ringing from the crazy things. Perhaps, if Moose had been the type to keep track of old wives' tales, he would have thought that his ears were ringing because someone was thinking of him.

Someone was.

Bonnie Leigh was getting pretty sick of Dean Hanson and his rules. What did he think he was—God? He certainly acted like it, setting up rules for everybody and expecting everybody to follow them in blind obedience.

A case in point was the way Hanson took it upon himself to plan and arrange every single meeting. What was so great about him that he should be the leader every last time? For her money they ought to have a sort of rotating chairmanship, with everybody getting a chance to plan and direct a meeting. So what if a couple of the members got things a little loused up that way? She, for one, had some damned good ideas, a lot more imaginative and exciting than some of the junk Hanson came up with week after week. What made him so darned special?

But that wasn't the worst of it. The bad part was this "only on meeting nights" nonsense. Now how in the world was she supposed to get along with only having a boy once a week? It might have been all right if she wasn't used to it more often, but in the past months she had become so used to a steady supply of sex that she was damned if she was going to turn off her glands like a water faucet. It just couldn't go on like that.

Every once in a while she had a boy over to her house during the week anyway and to hell with Dean Hanson and his rules. But that wasn't enough either, for some unknown reason. She didn't quite know why, but it was getting so that nothing in the world seemed to be enough.

And, just two and a half weeks ago, three weeks come Saturday night, she did something she had never done before. She had sexual relations with a boy who wasn't in the club, a boy who did not live in Palmer.

Not a boy, really. A man this time, an honest-to-Christ man who was better than thirty years old. She found the man in Norcrosse, a larger town some twenty miles due north, and she found him quite deliberately. She met him in a bar, let him pick her up, went to his apartment with him and did everything he thought up for her to do.

She'd been back the next week. Not to him, not this time, because what he had to offer was not enough for her any more than were the offerings of the Unicorns. This time she wanted more than one man, after a brief tour of the bars, she managed to line up fourteen of them. She remembered that first night, the initiation night when all the male Unicorns had taken her, and she tried now to recapture that night. It was good, it was better than anything in a long time, it hurt and it ached and it was wonderful.

It was not quite enough.

Now she was in her bedroom lying on the bed that was the scene of a good many love bouts, lying on her bed and wondering how she would wait two more days before the meeting came, knowing already that the meeting itself would, like too many others, be far from satisfactory.

She thought of calling one of the Unicorns. Her folks wouldn't be home for two hours or more. But what good would that do? Nobody had satisfied her recently and they wouldn't manage now.

What would?

She got up from the bed, her hands shaking more than a little while she fumbled for a cigarette. She was smoking more than ever lately and the cigarettes never tasted good any more. Sometimes when she awoke in the morning her mouth tasted as though the world was using it for an ashtray, just as it sometimes appeared as though the world was using another portion of her anatomy for the disposition of another sort of material.

She got the cigarette going after her shaking hands wasted two matches in succession. Then she took a few deep drags, purposely taking in so much smoke that she had to cough. She was punishing herself with the cigarettes and she knew it.

Now what?

The cigarette wasn't helping. She needed something, needed something badly, needed something desperately, so desperately that any minute now she was going to start climbing the walls, screaming and tearing her hair and shrieking her lungs out and squealing like a stuck pig and wailing and yowling and—

Steady. She had to get a grip on herself, had to calm down or she was going to flip completely. By a sheer act of will—one that was becoming increasingly familiar and decreasingly effective— she forced herself to relax, forced her nerves to stop jangling quite so violently, forced her hands to quit shaking.

She had to call somebody, had to get someone over or she wouldn't be able to stand it. And it had to be someone in the club because there was no one else she could call on. Now all she had to do was figure out who it could be, who she could call and who could come the closest to bring her what she needed, whatever in the world it might turn out to be, whatever it was she had to have or go mad.

Dean was out. He wouldn't come, would raise hell with her and it would be all over. She ran the others through her mind—Jack Lacey, Ray Saltonstall, Ed Bainbridge, Larry Prince, Chuck Folsom, Alan Marshall, Dave Carson. Each in turn she rejected, each in turn offered no promise of any genuine or near-genuine fulfillment.

Until she came to Marv Gardens.

He was the one, and even with him she could not be at all certain, but he was the one if anyone was to be the one. The last time with him had been good, quite good, and she sensed intuitively that this time would be better, that there was something tied up within Moose Gardens that she needed. There had been little hints of it all along that only now were dropping into the proper perspective. She thought about Marvin Gardens, thought about what they would do when he came to her, and already the beads of sweat were emerging from her pores and the little hairs bristling on the nape of her neck.

She stubbed her cigarette out viciously, ground it to shreds and hopped off the bed and hurried down the stairs to the phone. Her fingers were trembling slightly when she dialed his number but she managed to get all the digits right and managed to keep her voice almost calm when he answered the phone and she spoke to him.

"Moose? This is Bonnie. Why don't you drop over this afternoon?"

"Well, I—"

"C'mon," she coaxed. "I'd really like to see you. I want to see you a lot, Moose."

"I've got . . . a lot of work, Bonnie. I don't honestly think—"

She coaxed, she pressed on, she pushed and prodded and got rid of his excuses, and when even that wasn't working, when extreme hesitation on his part had the opposite effect of heightening her excitement still more, she began to promise him just what she would do, just how good she would be, just how much she wanted him to come over and just how appreciative she would feel towards him as soon as he arrived.

And, of course, he agreed.

Satisfaction and tingling excitement were mingled in equal portions as she waited for him. She first went up to her room and undressed, preparing her slim body for his possession of it, putting on a thin nightie of sheer black nylon, coming downstairs and sitting and waiting for him. And, although her conscious mind never stated the fact to herself or to the world, she knew inside, way down deep inside just what it was that he promised and just what it was that she wanted from him.

Pain.

He did not want to see Bonnie. He wanted not at all to see Bonnie and he must have made that relatively obvious to her over the telephone, but in the end she had won and he had lost. And now he was on his way over there, over to her house to see her and take her as she wanted him to, and fear ran through his bloodstream and matched the hunger that she had planted there.

He was afraid. Moose Gardens was a big boy and he feared few things, but now he was afraid, afraid of and for Bonnie Leigh, afraid of and for himself. The fear didn't grip icily; instead it burned like hellfire and, perversely, made him walk faster than usual as he headed toward the house where Bonnie lived.

The switchblade knife, with seven cold inches of keen steel ready to spring to attention at an instant's notice, nestled uncomfortably in the pocket of his blue jeans. He could feel it against his thigh as he walked and it felt cold, deadly.

And he was afraid.

His mind told him to go home, to throw the knife into a sewer, to for Christ's sake do something before something went horribly fearfully wrong. But he kept walking—if anything he walked still faster.

And the knife, the goddamn knife, stayed right where it was, right there in his goddamn pocket.

He walked up the path to her door without wanting to and hesitated before ringing her bell. He really hesitated just then and it is quite possible that, if her door had not opened without his ringing the bell, he might have turned away and left her to squirm in silent agony. But this is not for us to contemplate—we can only recall Trevelyan's words about the impossibility of testing an historical fact. In this case it is an historical fact that Bonnie had been waiting for him, that she saw him coming and that she opened the door.

He entered.

The door closed.

He saw her in her black nightie that he could see through and he wanted to rip it off her, to tear the thing into pieces and to rip the pieces into shreds. He had to fight to keep his hands at his sides and when she came to him and rubbed up against him it was even harder for him to control himself. But he did, and he followed in silence as she led him upstairs. He walked behind her, and as he watched her cute little behind sway from side to side while she ascended the staircase, his fingers automatically dipped into his pocket and closed around his knife.

Inside her room, with its door closed and its four walls isolating them, she turned and smiled up at him, her eyes hot and her body tantalizing.

"Won't your folks—"

"They won't be home for hours."

"But—"

"Hurry up!"

She took off the nightie and waited, naked, while he removed his own clothes. When he took off his pants he took the knife from his pocket and held it in his right hand in such a manner that she could not see it. He didn't know why he took the knife from his pocket. But he could not help it.

He was afraid, very much afraid, very desperately and horribly afraid. He looked at her, looked at her lovely little breasts and her sensuous hips and her face drawn in passion and his heart swelled up and scared him it was beating so violently. She looked at him and he looked at her, two naked high school students staring at each other like knights at a vision of the Holy Grail, and he knew that something horrible was surely going to happen and prayed that somehow it wouldn't, that some way or other God would be good to him and everything would turn out all right.

Neither of them moved; neither of them spoke for the longest minute in the history of the world. When he spoke, finally, his voice came out sounding like the voice of a castrated bull frog on a very cold and rainy night.

"What . . . what do you want me to do?"

A soft pause, tense and electric. Then her mind spoke through her mouth and her own words astounded her as much as they astounded him. They were what she felt and they came without her asking them. They were spoken in a soft and gentle voice but they sounded as though an English-speaking cannon had been shot off in the stillness of the room.

Bonnie Leigh said: "I want you to hurt me."

It was a command and he responded to it as such. What he did was done without his willing it, without his even realizing it, automatically and effortlessly and altogether inevitably. He acted like a well-trained machine and his body did things without his mind instructing it.

With his left hand he punched her in the mouth. The hand came up in a sweeping roundhouse hook that almost lifted her into the air. She fell sprawling on the bed, her mouth open in an uncomprehending O and her eyes wide.

He was still using his left hand when he picked up one of the two blue pillows at the head of her bed and clamped it over her face. He held it not so tightly that she could not breathe but tightly enough so that when she screamed the scream was muffled by the pillow and inaudible to anyone but he himself. Not completely inaudible, because he wanted to hear her scream.

Now she began to struggle. She flailed the air with her bare legs. Then he heaved himself onto the bed and sat on her legs, planting his huge bulk on top of her thighs, and then she did not struggle any more.

Up until now he had been using his left hand. That was because the knife, the seven-inch switchblade, was still gripped tightly in his right hand.

Now it was time to use his right hand.

He pressed the button and the knife came alive in his hand. He stared at it, then stared at her milk-white breasts, then at the knife a second time and then once more at her breasts.

He drew a thin red line on one breast and the pillow throbbed like a broken heart beneath his left hand.

He drew another red line on the other breast. This line was thicker because the point of the knife penetrated somewhat deeper.

He looked at the blood.

And at the knife.

And at her flat pale stomach.

And drew another line.

Outside the sun was shining and birds were singing and the grass was getting greener with the full force of spring. Men worked and children played and worms turned. It was a good day outside.

Inside it was not. It was a bad day, a very bad day.

After the third red line had appeared on Bonnie Leigh's stomach, Marvin Gardens had no idea what happened. He did not know what was happening while it was happening and he did not remember what had happened after it had happened. Everything that had been bottled up was suddenly spilling out and he participated in the spilling-out process without knowing what was going on.

Bonnie Leigh did not know what was going on either. After the third red line had appeared on her stomach she mercifully passed out. So, in truth, no one knew what happened there. Later on the coroner of the county made some assertions and coupled them with some guesses, but by that time no one really cared any more.

It wasn't very nice to think about.

Five minutes?

Or twenty minutes? Or an eternity?

Five minutes or twenty minutes or an eternity after it was over, five minutes or twenty minutes or an eternity after Bonnie Leigh got her wish and Marvin Gardens fulfilled his destiny, Marvin Gardens suddenly realized just what he had done, just what had happened to him.

He reacted quite strangely.

First of all, he wiped the blood from his seven-inch switchblade knife, folded the blade back into the handle and placed the knife gingerly on top of Bonnie Leigh's maple dresser. He was very compulsive in wiping the knife, but he did not take the trouble to remove the blood from his own body or to straighten up the room in any way whatsoever.

Instead he got dressed. He dressed slowly and neatly, although blood on his chest soaked through the front of his shirt, and when he was fully dressed he picked up the knife once more and returned it to his pants pocket.

Then he walked downstairs, lifted the telephone receiver to his ear, and dialed a number.

Dean Hanson answered.

"This is Moose, Dean."

"What's the good word, fellow?"

A deep breath. Then, flatly: "No good word, Dean. I'm over at Bonnie's house."

"I see."

"And I need your help."

"Can't handle Bonnie all by yourself? You surprise me, fellow. I'd have expected—"

"Dean," he cut in. And then, after a pause, he said: "I've just . . . killed Bonnie."

Silence from the other end of the line for perhaps a second. Then Moose was explaining everything that he could remember in a lifeless monotone, talking steadily and flatly to the vacuum on the other end of the wire.

"And I need help," he finished.

"Help? What do you mean?"

"Well . . . the club, Dean. Everything will get all mixed up. I mean we're all in this and—"

"What club?"

"The Unicorns. What do you think I'm talking about? Look, Dean, I—"

"Unicorns? I'm afraid I don't understand what you're talking about, Marvin. If you could be a little bit more explicit—"

For a thoroughly hysterical second Moose thought that (a) there was no club and (b) he was in a dream that somebody else was having.

Then he got the message.

"Dean—"

A slight pause. Then: "I'm sorry, Mr. Gardens, but I'm quite busy this afternoon. Unless you have something to tell me that makes a certain amount of sense I'm afraid I'll have to conclude this conversation."

"Oh," Moose said. "So that's how it's going to be. I get it."

A longer pause.

Then, softly, "Sorry, Moose. But that's how it's going to be."

A hollow click.

The line was dead and he replaced the receiver with empty eyes and arms that weighed a ton each.

He remained in the living room for twenty minutes. Then, like a figure out of a comic opera, he decided to make a quick getaway. He leaped out of his chair, dashed out the door, and ran into the corpulent figure of Mr. Reginald Leigh.

"Why, Marvin! Is something the matter?"

A wild impulse to get the knife once more from the trouser pocket came and went instantly. He did nothing; he stood with his mouth open and the blood showing through his shirt and a flat and empty look in his flat and empty eyes.

"Marvin? What's wrong, Marvin? Is something the matter with Bonnie? Is Bonnie all right?"

The heavy-set man was holding him by the arm now and

Moose, who could have broken the man with a blow and who could have shaken the grip simply by shrugging away from it, stood limp as a strand of boiled spaghetti.

And then, suddenly, he began to cry like an infant.

CHAPTER 20

"I don't know anything about a club like that," Betty Jo Meltzer said. "Honest. I don't know a thing about it. I never even heard of such a thing."

The County Sheriff, a hawk-nosed man with piercing blue eyes, snorted. He seemed about to say something but the Palmer Police Chief cut him off.

"Thanks, Betty Jo," the Chief said. "I'm sorry if we troubled you."

Betty Jo Meltzer walked off and disappeared. The Chief made a notation on a pad of ruled yellow paper. He studied the notation, looked at it as though it contained some shred of hidden truth, and raised his eyes to those of the Sheriff.

"You're a damn fool," the Sheriff advised him. "But I suppose you know that."

"Matter of opinion," the Chief said.

"The hell it is. The girl was lying same as all the rest of 'em so far have been lying. Lying in her teeth and all you got to do is throw her a curve and she'll crack. Crack like cement with too much sand in it."

"Maybe."

"Maybe be damned. It's a sure thing."

"I'm in charge of this," the Chief reminded him.

"You're still behaving like a damned fool."

"Maybe," said the Chief. "And maybe you're the damned fool. Ever look at it that way?"

"How do you figure?"

"What have we got?" the Chief asked. "We've got the Gardens boy who just got finished cutting the Leigh girl into so many pieces that all the king's horses and all the king's men couldn't do the necessary patchwork on her. We've got a story out of him that looks like a fairy tale—"

"Except it ain't."

"Except it ain't. Except he has to be telling the truth because he couldn't lie if he wanted to. And he doesn't want to, so he's telling the truth."

"Then why in the—"

"Hold up a minute, will you? We've got a story about a sex club called the Unicorns or some such fanciful name and we've got a list of seventeen kids besides this Gardens boy who are supposed to be mixed up in it. And they're guilty as all get out and they're not saying a word."

"If you'd just put it right to 'em," the Sheriff exploded. "If you'd just put it right to 'em and hit 'em hard with it they'd crack into bits. If—"

"Shut up for a minute, will you? Goddamn it if you don't run off at the mouth like an old woman. Just because you have to run for office where they have to appoint me don't mean you have to make your speeches to me. I don't feel like listening to them."

The Sheriff shut up.

"There's nobody in town like you for being so right and so wrong at the same time. If I put it right to 'em they'll crack," he parroted. "Can't you see a single damn thing? Can't you count and see there's one more girl than there is boys on the damn list? Can't you get it into your fat head that there's somebody left off this list?"

The Sheriff pursed his lips.

"If you used your head," the Chief went on, beginning to enjoy the whole affair, "you'd figure out that someone coached those kids. Every solitary damn one of them has the same story to the word. There's somebody on the outside who set the thing up and you can bet he's not a high school kid either. He's an older guy, and he's a first class son of a bitch, and when I get him you can bet I'm gonna kick his balls through the top of his head before I jail him."

The Sheriff thought for a minute. "Mebbe," he said.

"Maybe," said the Chief with relish, "be damned."

"Not saying there ain't, but if there is this guy, why didn't the Gardens boy mention him?"

"Couldn't."

"Couldn't! He cracked so wide you could walk through him. Why in the name of—"

"Couldn't," the Chief repeated. "Same as he couldn't tell why he done it to the Leigh girl. Doesn't know, doesn't remember, all knots inside."

"Well," said the Sheriff. He thought for a long moment, then said: "So what in hell are we doing now?"

"Waiting."

"What for?"

"For a kid to crack all by his lonesome," the Sheriff said. "For a crack-up that comes by itself so that nothing gets left out of it.

Because I don't much care if a passel of brats stand on their heads and screw each other's brains out. It's when some son of a bitch who ought to know better steps in that I want to get him. I want to get him and nail him to the damned wall."

Ed Bainbridge had a chair to himself in a room by himself while he waited for them to get around to calling him as they were calling each of the Unicorns in turn. In the privacy of the room he cursed himself in silence for (a) not going to Mr. Schwerner with the whole mess the minute he heard about it, (b) ever getting mixed up with it at all, and (c) not cutting his throat with a razor once he was in.

Soon, he thought, they would call him. And soon, he knew, he would have to decide what he was going to tell them. Hanson, of course, had called and handed him and everybody else a story. He knew that the others were going to hew the line.

But he was damned if he knew what he was going to do.

The smartest thing, he guessed, was to do just what the others were doing, no more and no less. According to Hanson, all they could have was Moose's word and Moose was nutty as a fruitcake and everybody knew it. If they just kept telling the same story over and over it didn't matter what anybody else thought. Even if the police knew they were lying, nobody had a charge to press against them and nobody had a grain of evidence.

As long as they all kept their mouths shut.

That was one argument. And there was another argument which Hanson hadn't even bothered to use but which had come quickly enough to Ed. Simply, what good would it do to show the whole thing up now? All it could do was louse up everybody in the club for good, and for what? Moose would get the same treatment anyway, Bonnie would remain every bit as dead, and who would profit?

Nobody.

It was hard, Ed Bainbridge thought, and he did not know what course to take, did not know at all. He rested his head in his hands, waiting for them to call him, hoping somebody would crack before it was up to him, hoping that whichever course he picked when it was his turn, that it would be the right course, that it would be the best thing for everybody, and that, somehow, he could come out of the whole thing without hating himself any more bitterly than he already did.

Mary Hobson had been crying and her cheeks were stained with tears. Now she was all cried out. She too sat on her own chair in her own private waiting room, waiting for them to come down the hall for her and ask her the questions.

She was just beginning to realize what had happened.

First and foremost, the girl who had for a long time been her best friend in the world was dead. Bonnie Leigh was dead, dead, dead—she would never walk around or talk or . . . or do anything at all. And she had not died quickly, mercifully in an accident, nor had she died slowly and sensibly from a disease. She had been murdered, brutally murdered, and what's more Mary knew the murderer just as she had known the girl who was murdered, and the whole situation was so horrible that even realizing just what had happened she still could not come anywhere near to grasping the enormity of it.

Already she took it for granted—and did not care—that she would be thrown out of school, disowned by her family, deserted by every acquaintance she had ever had. Already she was firmly convinced that her life would be hell from now until her death, and that if there was an afterlife she would spend it in a hell especially designed for her.

This, strangely, she could accept. Perhaps her ability to accept it is an index of the depths to which she had sunk; paradoxically, perhaps it is a sign of deep and abiding strength of character. Or perhaps it is neither of these, perhaps it is nothing more or less than her particular reaction to a traumatic experience to which no particular importance or significance ought to be attached.

What bothered her more than anything else was the battery of questions she would have to face at any moment.

And, and again this is strange, she began to think of Ed. While she did not know whether to lie or to tell the truth to the police, whether or not to deviate from the line Hanson had sketched so elaborately for her, she felt that of all of them Ed alone might be the one to tell the truth, for better or for worse.

She hoped two things:

She hoped that Ed would tell them the truth. Whether or not it was right that way, whether or not it was better that way—these things were suddenly irrelevant. She wanted them to know and she wanted Ed to tell them.

And, secondly, she wanted them to call Ed before they called her.

Because she was afraid to lie or to tell the truth, to step forward or backward or even to stay where she was. She was afraid, afraid because she felt that whatever she did it would be the wrong thing the moment she did it. She did not want to have to decide for herself.

The Sheriff took his pipe from the pocket of his windbreaker and dipped it into a leather pouch of white burley tobacco. He tamped the tobacco into the large bowl in the manner of a man who is elaborately forcing himself to remain patient. Then he scratched a wooden match on the sole of his shoe and lit the pipe, taking a good deal of time in the process so that the pipe was lit evenly all the way across.

He puffed three times on the pipe.

He said: "I don't see where we're getting at."

"Patience," said the Chief.

The Sheriff puffed more slowly on the pipe. The smoke he released from between slightly parted lips was heavy and dense and it drifted in grey amorphous gobs to the ceiling. The two of them watched it without saying anything.

"Damn," the Sheriff said. "Every last one of them with the same damn story."

The Chief nodded.

"Every last one."

"I know it," the Chief said. "I told you it'd be like that. I told you they'd get one story that the son of a bitch handed them on a silver platter. Now they're stuck with it and they don't know what to do."

"So where does that put the two of us?"

The Chief shrugged. "Not so bad off," he said. "We got two more of them to go, the Hobson girl and the Bainbridge boy. Assuming they stay clammed up like the rest, then we send the whole batch of 'em home."

"Older you get the dumber you get."

The Chief stared at him. The Sheriff held his gaze for a few seconds, then lowered his eyes and puffed furiously at his pipe.

"Then we pick them up again in the morning," he went on. "Then we ask them the same questions in the same tone of voice, and we keep doing it until one of them cracks. Which, if it don't happen by tomorrow morning, you can kick my butt clear up to Boston."

"You say tomorrow morning?"

The Chief nodded.

"Hell," the Sheriff said. "Hell, I just might take you up on that little thing."

"Your privilege."

"You say clear to Boston?"

"Clear to Boston."

"That's a hell of a ways to get your rear kicked, you know. You figure you got everything pretty well figured out, eh?"

"Hell," the Chief said, "I'm hardly sitting here begging to have my ass kicked."

"You must have it figured," the Sheriff said. "You were never one to stick your neck out."

"Or my ass."

"Or your ass," the Sheriff agreed. "I sure as hell hope you're right."

• • •

Marvin Gardens was not sitting on a chair in a room. He was instead lying on a cot in a cell. He was in a straitjacket and he could not move. He would not have wanted to move even if he could have.

At the moment his mind was quite literally a blank. He had lapsed into something resembling catatonia, and while images no doubt flowed through his sick brain, no one else could ever know what he was thinking about. This catatonic state was by no means constant; from time to time he would achieve moments of semi-lucidity in which he would remember old football plays, old blocks and tackles, old Saturday afternoons with the cheerleaders shouting and Saturday evenings with the girls worshipping him.

But not now.

Now only the fog that obscured everything, only the soft blanket of catatonia with a sweet pink smell to it and the taste of mothers' milk.

If he had been able to think, if he could have enjoyed the blessings of catatonic escape and the life of rationality at once, he would have realized that both he and the girl he had murdered were, in fact, the fortunate ones.

They had escaped.

"Well?"

"I don't know," said the Chief. "Two of them left and we might as well take one as the other. Ed Bainbridge and Mary Hobson left and I suppose one's as good as the next. What do you say?"

The Sheriff shrugged. "Hardly matters. Neither one's gonna crack, not for tonight. Take your choice—I don't care one way or the other."

The Chief scratched his head. "Ought to pick one or the other," he mumbled, half to himself and half to the Sheriff. "Seems as though it might make a difference."

"How?"

The Chief thought it over. "Guess it can't," he said at length. "Don't see how it could."

The Chief thought again, this time more briefly.

"You're right," he said.

"So who'll it be?"

The Chief thought, this time only for a second, and then he threw back his head and laughed. The laugh, however, was mirthless.

"Damned if I'm gonna decide," he said. "I'm gonna walk down that hallway and take the first one I come to and to blazes with it."

The First One He Came To stood up when the Chief entered the room. The Chief smiled, an altogether appealing smile, and motioned to the First One.

"Want to come this way?"

The First One He Came To followed. Footsteps were loud on the concrete floor of the station house. Air was thick with smoke and fear. The First One was afraid, very much afraid. and sick inside, very sick inside, and the First One was still not at all sure.

The two of them entered the room. The Chief returned to his seat beside the Sheriff and pointed to the room's third chair.

"Have a seat," he suggested.

The First One sat down.

Eyes flashed, each person taking in each in turn. Time did not stand still so much as it ceased to exist as a realistic dimension.

The Sheriff was lighting his pipe again, taking his time with the process as usual, although this time the ceremony cloaked suspense rather than impatience. The Chief lit a cigarette, started to return the pack to his pocket and then thought better of it. He extended the pack to the Witness, who shook his head.

Then, levelly, the Chief said: "You wouldn't happen to know anything about a group that calls themselves the Unicorns, would you?"

The Witness, without a pause, said: "Yes."

The Sheriff dropped his pipe, although he later insisted that it merely slipped from his grip.

The Chief did not bat an eyelash.

"Really?"

"Yes," said the witness. "I've been a member."

"Care to tell us about it?"

"Yes," said Ed Bainbridge. "That's what I want to do."

They found Dean Hanson in his own home which, all in all, was quite appropriate. When he opened the door the Chief of Police and the Sheriff gave the door a shove, stepped inside and closed it behind them.

Hanson was smooth, calm, ostensibly relaxed. He was wearing a plaid smoking jacket and a pair of Italian silk pants.

"You have a warrant, Chief?"

"No," said the Chief gravely. "Come to think of it, I don't have a warrant."

Hanson turned to the Sheriff. "Then you must have the warrant," he suggested. "You can't invade a man's privacy without a warrant."

"Hell," the Sheriff said. "Now how in the name of the lord did I ever forget the warrant? It beats the blazes out of me."

"Look," Hanson said. "Now you—"

The Chief of Police hit Hanson in the face. There was a satisfying crunch of bone and the lean, long-haired man fell to his knees.

The Sheriff hit Hanson full in the mouth. Teeth gave way. Hanson fell flat on the floor now, his nose broken, his mouth a bloody mess.

"Damn," said the Chief. "I'm damn near the only police officer in the New England region who's a civil liberties union member and look at me now."

"Police brutality," the Sheriff said.

"A hell of a note," the Chief said.

Hanson was unconscious.

"What now?"

"Now," said the Chief of Police, "we load him into the car and drive out into the country."

"Makes good sense," said the Sheriff. He picked up Hanson, tossed him over one shoulder and headed toward the car parked outside. The Chief of Police watched him until he was out the door. Then he began searching the house.

As he had suspected there was nothing whatsoever to be found. He looked for everything the Unicorns had described, knowing in advance that Hanson by now had removed and destroyed every trace of evidence. But there was no question about its existence. The separate testimony of every one of the kids, their will broken with relief once they heard that the cat was out of the bag, was enough to convince everybody. The Chief of Police had no doubt that it would convince a court as well, but the thought of dragging all those kids into court wasn't very pleasant.

The Chief took a deep breath, then walked out of the house. He knew it was nothing more than his imagination but the air seemed infinitely cleaner and fresher outside of the house.

He walked to his car and saw that the Sheriff had Hanson sprawled across the back seat.

"Nope," he said. "Not in my car, damn it. He rides in the trunk."

"He'll rattle around one hell of a lot."

"Let him," the Chief said. "I don't haul garbage in my back seat. Car's only five years old. Got a good five years left in it. No sense filthying up the back seat."

They put him in the trunk.

Before long they were far enough out of town and the Chief of Police told the Sheriff to pull off the road. He did and they got out of the car. They opened the trunk and hauled Hanson out of it. He was groggy but conscious.

"You can't do this," he said through broken teeth. "You do this and you're in trouble."

The Sheriff nodded solemnly. "What are you fixing to do?" he asked the Chief.

"Told you before," the Chief said. "Told you I was going to kick him in the balls until they came out the top of his head."

After three thoroughly satisfying attempts, the Chief came to the unhappy conclusion that the precise feat he was trying to accomplish was biologically out of the question.

"Hell," he said. "Can't be done."

"Damned good try, though."

"Thanks," the Chief said. "Got anything you feel like doing?"

"Nope."

"Hell," said the Chief. He drew a .45 caliber pistol from his pocket, placed the mouth against Hanson's head, and solemnly blew his brains out. Then he wiped off the pistol and threw it into the tall grass a ways off the road.

"I'll be damned," said the Sheriff. "Poor old Hanson got himself killed."

"Looks that way," the Chief admitted.

"Must have been a syndicate killing," the Sheriff said. "You hear a lot about those boys. I hear tell they operate along these lines. Bring a guy in from nowhere, have him do a job and then put him on a train and send him away before the police officers know just what's going on."

The Chief nodded. "You're right," he said. "If we look we'll probably find a gun hereabouts that can't be traced, no witnesses . . . it looks like this one's gonna be a tough one to solve."

"Damn tough."

"Hell," said the Chief. "I have a feeling this is gonna wind up one of those unsolved homicides."

"I get the same feeling," the Sheriff said.

And together they walked back to the car and drove more slowly back to the town of Palmer.

My Newsletter: I get out an email newsletter at unpredictable intervals, but rarely more often than every other week. I'll be happy to add you to the distribution list. A blank email to lawbloc@gmail.com with "newsletter" in the subject line will get you on the list, and a click of the "Unsubscribe" link will get you off it, should you ultimately decide you're happier without it.

Lawrence Block has been writing award-winning mystery and suspense fiction for half a century. You can read his thoughts about crime fiction and crime writers in *The Crime of Our Lives*, where this MWA Grand Master tells it straight. His most recent novels are *The Girl With the Deep Blue Eyes*; *The Burglar Who Counted the Spoons*, featuring Bernie Rhodenbarr; *Hit Me,* featuring Keller; and *A Drop of the Hard Stuff,* featuring Matthew Scudder, played by Liam Neeson in the film *A Walk Among the Tombstones.* Several of his other books have been filmed, although not terribly well. He's well known for his books for writers, including the classic *Telling Lies for Fun &f Profit,* and *The Liar's Bible.* In addition to prose works, he has written episodic television (*Tilt!*) and the Wong Kar-wai film, *My Blueberry Nights.* He is a modest and humble fellow, although you would never guess as much from this biographical note.

Email: lawbloc@gmail.com
Twitter: @LawrenceBlock
Facebook: lawrence.block
Website: lawrenceblock.com